William Schwenck Gilbert

The Ne`er Do Weel

Comedy drama in three acts

William Schwenck Gilbert

The Ne`er Do Weel
Comedy drama in three acts

ISBN/EAN: 9783744786782

Printed in Europe, USA, Canada, Australia, Japan

Cover: Foto ©Andreas Hilbeck / pixelio.de

More available books at **www.hansebooks.com**

THE

"NE'ER DO WEEL."

A

COMEDY DRAMA IN THREE ACTS,

BY

W. S. GILBERT.

—

THE PROPERTY OF

E. A. SOTHERN, Comedian.

. —

Dramatis Personæ.

—o—

MR. SETON (*of Drumferry*).

GERARD SETON (*his son*).

JEFFERY ROLLESTONE (*a vagabond*).

CAPTAIN O'HARA (*a retired merchant-sailor*).

RICHARD QUILT (*Mr. Seton's discharged secretary*).

JAKES (*a butler*).

DAVID (*O'Hara's gardener*).

MARION CALLENDAR (*a wealthy widow*).

MISS PARMINTER (*a distant connection of Mr. Seton's*).

JESSIE O'HARA (*O'Hara's niece*).

ACT I.—A Ruined Watermill, near O'Hara's cottage.

(*Three Months' Interval between Acts 1 and 2*).

ACT II.—Library at Drumferry.

(*One Night's Interval between Acts 2 and 3*).

ACT III.—Interior of O' Hara's cottage.

DATE.—THE PRESENT DAY.

ACT I.

SCENE. *The bank of a river, with boat-house* L. *The river (indications of which are seen from the front) is supposed to run diagonally across the back of the stage from* 2 E L, *until it is lost in the cloth. At the back (*R C*) is a picturesque ruined watermill—the wheel of which is so situated as to appear to dip into the river. The access to the mill is from a platform on its right, raised some six or eight feet above the stage, and masked by rockwork and shrubs. It is accessible from* 3 E R. *There is a rough (but easily practicable) natural descent from the platform to the stage.* CAPTAIN O'HARA'S *cottage* R.

CAPTAIN O'HARA *is discovered fishing, from the bank.*

O'H. Bother the fish, *I* say. These here rivers, with a strong six-knot stream in 'em, don't give a trout time to catch sight of the fly, much less rise to it. Ah! give me trawling for *my* money!

Enter QUILT.

QUILT. Good morning, Captain O'Hara.

O'H. Good mornin', Mr. Quilt.

QUILT. Any sport, Captain O'Hara?

O'H. Devil a bit, Mr. Quilt.

QUILT. Never mind. They say there's as good fish In the river, as ever came out of it, Captain O'Hara.

O'H. So there may be, for anything I've done to prevent it, this mornin' Mr. Quilt.

QUILT. Don't you think your fly's rather large, Captain O'Hara?

O'H. No, I don't, Mr. Quilt. The trout are travelling express, and when trout travel express they like the names of the stations printed big. If the fly was too small it might try their eyesight, Mr. Quilt. No, no; there can't be any mistake about the fly, for I made it myself. It's a fly I wouldn't take anything for. (*Showing a very large and clumsy fly.*)

QUILT. It's a fly you won't take anything *with*.

O'H. And how's Mr. Seton to-day? (*Putting up his tackle.*)

QUILT. I can't say, Captain O'Hara. Mr. Seton and I have parted company.

O'H. No!

QUILT. Yes. I resigned the secretaryship last night.

O'H. And what was that for?

QUILT. It's a very painful matter, Captain O'Hara. He got it into his head that there was something wrong with my accounts, and he had the impertinence to say that, if I didn't leave the house that minute, he'd kick me out of it. So of course I resigned. Mr. Seton never liked me.

O'H. No, my lad, he never did. He used to say you were so underhanded.

QUILT. But you stood up for me, Captain O'Hara?

O'H. In coorse. Tom O'Hara's not the man to stand by and hear an old chum abused, without putting in a good word for him. No, no. "He's a sneaking fellow, and I can't trust him," says Mr. Seton. "Granted," says I. "He *is* sneaking, but he's got a wonderful head for accounts." "But he's such a confounded liar," says he. "Granted again," says I.

"He *do* lie, but he writes the best hand in the county."
And so you do, my boy. (*Shaking* QUILT'S *hand heartily.*)

QUILT. I'm sure I'm much obliged to you, Captain O'Hara.

O'H. Not a bit. I always stand up for a friend; not but what I may seem odd times to be going against him. But that's only my cunning. If you want to gain your end never contradict flatly. Pull up short and snap goes your hawser. Pay out a bit before you belay, and you may hold on with a packthread. You see (*winking*), betwixt you and me, I expect Lord Dunveggan is goin' to put me on the Commission of the Peace one of these days, on Mr. Seton's recommendation, and I don't want to offend him.

QUILT. I hope Miss Jessie's pretty well.

O'H. Well, she's a bit down-hearted. She's going with her mother to London to day, and she don't like leaving me. She don't know anyone in London to speak of, and—"Oh, uncle, it'll be so lonely," says she. "Granted," says I, "it *will* be lonely, and very like you'll be treated unkind, and you'll fret and cry a good deal, I dessay, and with reason; but London's a fine place for getting on. Look at Whittington!" But that reflection didn't seem to cheer her up.

QUILT. Captain O'Hara, I wish I could get Miss Jessie to like me better.

O'H. I don't think you will.

QUILT. If you could bring yourself to speak a word for me, perhaps she might be brought to think more kindly of me.

O'H. I don't know. I don't think it's likely. If *I* was a pretty young gal and you asked me to marry you, I'd see you hanged first, and I don't believe I would then. Only, mind you, if I was a pretty young gal.

QUILT. But why, Capt. O'Hara?

O'H. Well, in the first place, a young gal looks for a good looking husband. Now you ain't good looking, are you?

QUILT. No, Capt. O'Hara, I'm afraid I'm not.

O'H. I'm sure you're not. Then a young gal looks for an agreeable husband. Now your dearest friend can't say you're agreeable, can he?

QUILT. I try very hard to be agreeable.

O'H. So I've remarked, my lad, but nature's too many for you. You've many good points—you've a rare head for timber—and for valuations and such like, I don't know your equal. But you ain't agreeable.

QUILT. I don't know what to do, I'm sure. Here she comes. If you'd only speak a good word for me—

O'H. My boy, I'll do what I can.

Enter JESSIE *from cottage.*

O'H. Jessie, my bird, come here. Here's Mr. Quilt. You know Mr. Quilt?

JES. Oh, yes, uncle, I know Mr. Quilt.

O'H. He's just been kicked out of Mr. Seton's house, because there's something wrong with his accounts, and he's very downhearted about it, poor fellow. Come--say a word to comfort him. He's very fond of you, Jessie.

JES. Oh, uncle, how can you?

O'H. Just so - how can I? (to QUILT) What did I tell you?

JES. I know nothing of Mr . Quilt—and its like his impertinence to think of such a thing.

O'H. Just so—it *is* like his impertinence.

QUILT. But Miss Jessie—don't decide rashly—hear me out—its only fair.

O'H. True. Fair play's a jewel. Hear him out, Jessie, and don't be rash.

Jes. Mr. Quilt, don't speak of it again. You've no right to say these things to me, when I tell you I don't want to hear them.

O'H. There's a good deal of truth in that.

Quilt. But if I don't speak again, you won't hear half of what I've got to say.

O'H. Well, come—that's reasonable, too.

Jes. Mr. Quilt, if you want me to speak plainly, I will do so. I do not like you, and that's the truth,

Quilt (*despondingly*). Nobody seems to like me, and I'm sure, I can't think why.

O'II. That's what *I* say! " He's such a disagreeable looking young man," people say, " True," says I. " but what's looks ?" " But he's such a dull dog." " True, again," says I—he's as dull as ditchwater —but his *mother's* a lady." Bless you, I've stood your friend, over and over again ; but people won't have you at any price. Come, Jess, if your box is packed, I'll have the trap put to, and drive you over to the station.

[*Exit* O'Hara *into cottage.*

Quilt. Miss Jessie, I know what this means. This is because of Mr. Gerard Seton.

Jes. What do you mean.

Quilt. Miss Jessie, I hate anything mean or underhanded, and it's my duty to tell you that I've got a secret of yours.

Jes. (*alarmed*). What secret ?

Quilt. I've found out, by the merest accident in the world, that you've been writing letters to that fellow.

Jes. Mr. Quilt !

Quilt. Yes, don't deny it, for he has a bundle of them in his bureau. Well, he left the key in it one day, and —well, I read some of them—just to see if I could believe my eyes—and I thought it my duty as an honourable man to tell you.

Jes. Mr. Quilt—you dared to read my letters? Your conduct is shameful, and I despise you more than I can say, You are a coward to say these things to me —do you hear ?—a mean and pitiful coward !

Quilt. Miss Jessie, when a gentleman's in love, he'll do anything mean and contemptible. He's cut me out, and I hate him for it. He means you no good, and I hate him for that. I a coward? Why I should like to see somebody kick him! A coward? Why, I could hear that he'd been poisoned with pleasure ! (Gerard *has entered, and overheard these last few lines.* Quilt *becomes aware of his presence, but, affecting not to see him, pretends that he was only repeating words used by someone else.*) "Yes, I could hear that he'd been poisoned with pleasure and satisfaction," says he. "I'll not hear Gerard Seton abused like that," says I. "He's hasty, but he's a gentleman to the backbone, and I won't hear a word against him." (*Turns round and sees* Gerard, *who carries a small portfolio.*) Dear me, Mr. Seton, I was not aware that I was overheard !

Ger. Is this fellow annoying you ? (*To* Jessie.)

Jes. Oh, yes—he has frightened me dreadfully !

Ger. Very good. Now sir, attend to me. I know you to be a dishonest vagabond—so I've no hesitation in speaking plainly to you. If you dare to address this young lady again, civilly or uncivilly, I'll come back from wherever I may be, and break every bone in your body.

Quilt (*with suppressed fury*). Mr. Gerard Seton —you be civil. Do you hear? You be civil. I know what I'm talking about—I know more than you think. So take care.   [*Exit* Quilt.

Ger. What does the scamp mean ?

JES. Why, he has read some of the letters I sent you—you ought to have been more careful. (GERARD *moves to follow him*). No, no—you mustn't go after him. Now, promise me you won't—at least, not now. After all, what does it matter?

GER. Not much, indeed—the letters are innocent enough, poor little woman! (*stroking her head*). Why, you've been crying!

JES. A little. Oh, Mr. Seton. I thought you were going to let me go away without saying good bye to me; and—and—I was a little donkey to think that, wasn't I? What have you got there? (*alluding to the portfolio*).

GER. I'm making a sketch of the old mill—I'm going to finish it now.

JES. Is it for me?

GER. Well, no—it's promised—

JES. To whom?

GER. To my cousin, Marion Callendar.

JES. Put it away—I don't want to see it. I'd rather not look at it.

GER. Why not?

JES. Because—because—Oh, Mr. Seton, I wish you had not kept my letters!

GER. My dear Jessie, I wish I had never had your letters.

JES. Why?

GER. Because, my dear little woman, I had no right to let you send them to me. I am older than you are, and I ought to have known better. But you were a child when you began to write to me, and they were such good little letters—and I could not foresee what would happen—it began so harmlessly. I never thought how it might end.

JES. It has ended by my loving you very dearly.

GER. My dear Jessie, I'm not a heartless cold-blooded scoundrel, though I'm a very vain foolish and thoughtless man—and what you have told me touches me very deeply—very deeply indeed. It was so plea-sant to be the confidant of all your little hopes and fears—so very, very pleasant—that I thought only of that, and I am terribly ashamed of myself. I am a poor man, and heavily in debt, and when I marry I must remember that. So, little woman, try and think of me as one who has done a very foolish thoughtless thing, and who is very sorry and very much ashamed.

JES. (*with suppressed emotion*). I am not angry—you have always been good and kind to me. I had no right to love you—but I couldn't help it—you never said one word to frighten me, or put me on my guard—you—you treated me with respect, and that is why I let myself love you. If it had been otherwise I should have despised and hated you, and my heart would not be breaking now—but you were good and kind and gentle—and oh, Mr. Seton, it seemed so natural to love you (*breaking down*).

GER. My dear little woman, love is a luxury that a poor man in my position can't afford. If he wants a wife, he must take a rich one, and if he finds that he can love her ever so little, why he may think himself a very lucky fellow.

JES. Is Mrs. Callendar very rich?

GER. What put Mrs. Callendar into your head?

JES. You—you are painting that picture for her.

GER. Come, Jessie, I'll tell you all about it. Mrs. Callendar *is* very rich. She is a very dear old friend, and, in fact, we have been brought up together like brother and sister. I—I am very much attached to Marion Callendar.

JES. Are you going to marry her?

GER. We have not come to that yet.

JES. But it *will* come to that?

GER. (*after a pause*). Perhaps.

JES. (*with a violent effort to control herself*). Then, Mr. Seton—I hope you will be happy—I do, indeed. Don't think of me, if it gives you pain. I did not expect you to love me. I am not angry—not a bit angry. I can't help crying, but I shall be better soon— it was my fault, but I could not help it—it seemed so natural. (*He is about to speak*). Please don't say anything to me. I would rather say " good bye," like this (*smiling through her tears*). Good bye, Mr. Seton. I can bear up. I shall often think of you—it was my fault— God bless you. Good bye. [*Exit* JESSIE *sobbing.*

GER. Poor little maid! I'd give a good round sum (if I had it) to undo the mischief I have done to her peace of mind. Such a good little girl, and such good little letters, so frank, and simple, and straightforward, and so badly spelt! I never guessed until a week ago that she cared for me. Thank God, there's no harm done after all. She'll soon forget me in London. But, by Jove, if I were a rich man and could afford to do as I liked, I don't know that I——. Bah! it's of no use to talk about that. I'm hard up, and we're all hard up, and Drumferry is mortgaged up to the crows' nests, so I shall make a reputable marriage with a young and wealthy widow, the requirements of society will be complied with, and the oldest family in the county will be spared the degradation of a *mésalliance*. And when a fellow's forced to marry for money, he may hold himself to be uncommonly lucky if he lights upon as good and loveable a woman as Marion Callendar.

(*During this soliloquy* GERARD *has been occupied in arranging a small portable easel, and in getting out his sketching materials.*

Enter Miss Parminter.

Miss P. Well, Mr. Seton, here we are at last, or rather here *I* am, for Marion is lagging behind to say "Good-bye" to the cottagers. How is the sketch getting on ?

Ger. Rather lamely. I'm not quite satisfied with it· When does Marion's train start ?

Miss P. At one o'clock. The carriage is to meet her here in half an hour. Ah, Mr. Seton, you will miss Marion sadly !

Ger. We shall all miss her, Miss Parminter.

Miss P. Mr. Seton, be frank with me.

Ger. Certainly, in what way ?

Miss P. Come, I am a very old friend, so I think I may be trusted. You and she are both leaving Drumferry to-day—you may not meet again for months. Tell me the truth about Marion.

Ger. Really, Miss Parminter, I ——

Miss P. Ah, Mr. Seton, this is a matter in which I am not easily deceived. I am a single woman with a great deal of spare time on my hands, and I have made a study of it.

Ger. Of what ? Of love ?

Miss P. No. The yearning of two young hearts towards each other I do not call "love." It is something too mysterious, too unearthly, too abstract for a word of four letters. I do not know, Mr. Seton, what the word is that I want—it should be a long word like climacteric—but whatever that word is, *that* I have made a study of. It is a fascinating pursuit, Mr. Seton.

Ger. I am sure it must be very interesting.

Miss P. Mr. Seton, it is absorbing. Ribald young men may laugh—they often do—but I care little for that. To be able to enter into the bosoms of one's

fellow creatures, and there listen, as it were, to the generally inaudible thrumming of their very heart-strings, is no light privilege, Mr. Seton.

GER. Indeed, you are very much to be envied, Miss Parminter.

MISS P. I think so, too. It is a great gift.

GER. Well, Miss Parminter, supposing, for the sake of argument, that I do admire my cousin very much, do you think, you who are so well qualified to judge, that there is any chance for me?

MISS P. Mr. Seton, I will be frank with you. That our dear Marion loves, I am very sure. That is a great point to have established, for having ascertained that, there only remains the question "Whom does she love?" which is of quite secondary importance.

GER. (*rather surprised*). Altogether insignificant!

MISS P. Exactly. Her symptoms are unmistake-able. She sighs much and eats little. If anything, it is the liver-wing of a chicken, which is always a significant joint, but more generally it is nothing. That she is affected by a recollection of the late Mr. Callendar I cannot believe, for, as you know, she married him against her will, and their married life was far from happy. I could mention many other symptoms, such as indifference about her back-hair, and a fidget-tiness during Divine service, and so forth; but they would convey no meaning to you who have not studied the subject. But be very sure that she loves.

GER. Miss Parminter, you have found out my secret. I am very much attached to Marion.

MISS P. I was sure of it.

GER. Now, what do you advise me to do? It's so awkward—we are such very old and intimate friends. If I were to take her hand and ask her if I might call her "Marion"—well, that would mean volumes if we were comparative strangers; but, situated as we are, it would smack of imbecility.

Miss P. Excuse me, Mr. Seton, but that would depend entirely upon how it was done. If you took her hand casually—like that—(*taking his hand carelessly*) it would (in your case) have no particular meaning, but if you took it (allow me, Mr. Seton, for one moment—I won't hurt you) like *that* (*taking his hand affectionately; looking pensively into his eyes*) the special significance of the action could not be misunderstood.

Ger. Miss Parminter, if I felt certain that she would not laugh at me——

Miss P. Have no fear. Leave it to me to ascertain diplomatically the state of her affections, before she leaves to-day. Will you leave it to me?

Ger. Indeed I shall be very, very much indebted to you.

Miss P. Then I'll do it, and you shall know the result this very morning.

Enter Marion Callendar.

Mar. Well, Gerard, did you think I was never coming? It takes so long to say " good bye " if you do it well, and I've made more friends during my six weeks' visit than I had any idea of. The old ladies I've kissed, the old gentlemen I've shaken hands with, and the little babies I've talked rubbish to! They were all so sorry that I'm going. I must be a very charming woman, Gerard.

Miss P. My dear Marion, that's exactly what Mr. Seton was saying when you arrived.

Mar. Thank you, but *he* didn't mean it. I *did*. So this is the old mill you are sketching for me.

Ger. Yes—it belonged to Waylett, the cornfactor, whose father and grandfather did a thriving trade with it years ago. But Waylett is ambitious, and he has

built a big warehouse, a mile below, with steam engines and hydraulic appliances, and deuce knows what, and so the old place has fallen into decay.

MAR. Poor old mill! You will laugh at me, I daresay, but do you know there is something very sad and solemn, too, and, very, very like the world, in the neglect with which the poor old-fashioned, broken-down old bread-winner is treated, now that the people who lived by it can do without it.

GER. It's the way of the world, Marion. How do you like the sketch?

MAR. It is capital, as far as it goes—but, my dear Gerard, it don't go far enough. That old mill bears a moral that is worth telling. Tell it, Gerard.

GER. But how?

MAR. (*considering*). Aye, how? Let me see—there should be a figure in the foreground—a figure that would point the touching lesson that it teaches. Now, what should that figure be?

MISS P. A broken-down old man, past work, and waiting for the end—whose friends have died around him, and left him here alone.

MAR. No—a broken-down *young* man—a man of capacity, but without energy—a man with a brain and a heart, but who has trusted entirely to impulse from without, to set them going—and who, that impulse having failed him, has sunk down, down, into a slough of poverty and wretchedness, from which his own nerveless grasp, will never, never, raise him.

GER. Yes; but that wants a model. I know a dozen loafing cads who would carry out your idea only too well, but you don't find them hereabouts.

MAR. A cad, as you call it, wouldn't do. He must be a gentleman at heart, but weak and wavering—a weathercock, whose lot in life depends on the shifting of the wind—and see. see, Gerard, there is the very man we want!

(JEFFERY ROLLESTONE *has appeared on the raised platform, and is seen leaning carelessly on a part of the woodwork, and throwing stones idly into the stream. His appearance is that of a man of thirty-five, poorly dressed in clothes that were once well-cut, careless, untidy and rather dissipated. Although his clothes are seedy, and his boots broken, and he shows very little linen, he has still the air of a broken-down gentleman. His linen is clean, though it is frayed at the cuffs.*)

GER. Poor devil! He looks hard-up enough at any rate!

MAR. Yes; his dress is poor and ragged, but he wears it well. He was once a gentleman I'll warrant. Don't you think so Miss Parminter?

MISS P. Decidedly. Mark my words, that man can tell a story.

GER. I'll be bound he can—a good many! Ten to one he's a swell-mobsman, but I'll use him for my sketch, and you and Marion can take a turn in the neighbourhood till I find out whether he is sober enough for you to listen to.

MAR. Gerard, you are very hard on the poor fellow. Do—do you think he would take money?

GER. I'm sure he would—if you left it about.

MAR. Nonsense. I mean would he take payment for sitting?

GER. I don't know. I think I can persuade him. At all events, I'll try.

MAR. Then give him half a sovereign, and make him happy for a day. Come along, Miss Parminter.

[Exeunt MARION *and* MISS PARMINTER.

GER. Happy for a day? Half a sovereign would

make him drunk for a week ! (*Hailing him.*) Hallo, you sir !

Rol. Hallo, *you* sir !

Ger. Have you half an hour to spare ?

Rol. Well, yes, I think so. I've an appointment with the Attorney-General at three, and unless I'm summoned by telegram to stand for the county, which may happen at any moment, I'm at liberty till then.

Ger. A funny dog, eh ? (*Contemptuously.*)

Rol. A funny dog, am I ? Oh, I dare say I am. I never looked at myself in that light before. Yes, I see what you mean. There's a humorous side to everything, even to ruin, and when you asked me if I had half an hour to spare, why, I suppose I felt it was pretty obvious that I had half a lifetime to spare if anybody wanted it ! Yes, I've half an hour to spare !

Ger. Do you feel inclined to earn half-a-sovereign ?

Rol. Ah ! I don't know—it's very warm, and I never work in the day time. I should like half-a-sovereign, too—if only for the novelty of the thing – but it's very warm. (*Coming down to stage*).

Ger. The fact is—I want a model.

Rol. Then don't take me—I haven't turned out well.

Ger. You see, I'm going to paint the old mill—

Rol. Not before its wanted.

Ger. And I have to introduce a figure. The mill is, as you see, a mere neglected ruin, and I want a loafing, broken-down, shabby-genteel, ne'er-do-weel in the foreground—

Rol. And you want me to sit for him—you think I'm the very thing—don't apologise—so I am.

Ger. (*rather confused*). Pardon me ; an artist does not expect to find exactly what he wants. He takes a suggestion and improves upon it. I don't want to reproduce *you*—I want a drunken, dissipated, good-for-nothing kind of fellow, and——

Rol. And when I'm "improved upon" you think I'll do.

Ger. You misunderstand me. There is a certain picturesque recklessness about you—a jolly devil-may-care independence—which, with a little assistance from the imagination—·

Rol. I know what you mean—I've remarked it myself. Not ten minutes since, as I was looking at my reflection in the stream (I took the liberty of allowing myself to be reflected in the stream—but it will wash out), I said to myself, "Jeff, my boy,—what is it that gives you that air of picturesque recklessness—·that convivial look of refined dissipation that is so generally remarked?" I think it must be something in the Lincoln and Bennett. I don't think Bennett was happy with the brim.

Ger. Well, you take your bad luck good-humouredly, at any rate.

Rol. Good-humouredly? Yes, I think I'm good-humoured. A man in my fix should try and keep his temper—if he can. A touchy or irritable man—or a stickler for personal comforts would not enjoy himself in my line of business. Yes, I make the best of things —and bad's the best. Were you ever hungry?

Ger. Hungry? Yes, often.

Rol. Aye, I know—on the moors when the man with the luncheon hasn't turned up. I don't mean that—I mean hunger without a grouse-pie in the background— and with no distinct prospect of staying it, to-day, to-night, or to-morrow. Hunger that eats *you*, for want of something better, till you feel like an excavated Stilton with the walls crumbling in. Hunger like that tries a touchy man—he gets fidgetty and irritable, and thinks

he's ill-treated. No—you want an even temper when you're on the tramp.

GER. Well, I wont detain you long. Throw your self on the grass, there, at the foot of that tree—so— now draw up the right leg, a little more, that'll do. (ROLLESTONE *does as directed*.) Can you smoke ? (GERARD *begins to sketch*.)

ROL. I don't know, I'll try (*takes out pipe case, opens it, produces a black pipe, and lights it*). Yes I *can* smoke.

GER. Then fire away. (GERARD *pauses*.) It's not quite what I want.

ROL. I'll tell you where I'm wrong, the line of my right leg is a continuation of my left arm, and cuts the picture diagonally. Now if I bend the leg and roll over —like that—you get some valuable curves.

GER. By Jove, that's true. I—I'm only an amateur.

ROL. So I see.

GER. You seem to know something of drawing.

ROL. Yes, I've met it ; a nodding acquaintance, nothing more. I know a good many professions in a " how-de-do, fine-day " sort of way.

GER. Why don't you work at one of them ?

ROL. Exactly. I often ask myself that. I say to my-self, " You've had a good education, and by birth you're a gentleman : why the devil don't you go into Parlia-ment, or get a Colonial governorship, or direct public companies, or marry an heiress, or start a bank ? By-the-bye you don't know of a snug little semi-detched banking concern going cheap, do you ?

GER. You're talking nonsense.

ROL. No; I beg your pardon—*your'e* talking non-sense. Work ? What am I to work at ? Why, look at me ! What are you painting ? A hopeless vaga-bond. And why did you ask me to sit to you ? Be-cause you saw at a glance, that I *am* a hopeless vagabond. And how is a poor devil with *that* stamped on every line of his face—on every rag of his wretched clothing—to find work that a—a—that a man of education can accept? Why the very dogs bark at me, damn them!

GER. I should be sorry to seem to ask an impertinent question—but it is evident to me, that you—that you were once in a very much better position—that, in short, you were at one time a—a—

ROL. A gentleman! Don't have any delicacy in applying the term to me. *I* haven't. Yes—I might have ruined half the tradesmen in Regent Street, once. Oh, yes. I was a gentleman, God help, me! I might have met you at dinner, whoever you are, and danced with your sister, whoever she is. Don't be angry—I danced devilish well!

GER. It's hard, I know, to rise, after a fall—I should be glad to help you to retrieve your position, if it lies in my power to do so.

ROL. Thanks, but it don't.

GER. That remains to be proved. Will you tell me your name?

ROL. No. Will you tell me yours?

GER. Yes. Gerard Seton.

ROL. Not the son of Seton of Drumferry, by any chance?

GER. Yes, I am Drumferry's son.

ROL. Good heavens! Why, let me look at you! Why, so it is! It's little Gerard Seton!

GER. You seem to know me very well.

ROL. (*mournfully.*) Yes. I know you very well, now. I had you in my mind not an hour since, but like a fool I thought of you as a boy — Gerard Seton! Why, haven't you made me out yet? No, you wouldn't. I am Jeffery Rollestone. Don't you remember me at Harrow?

GER. What! Why it is—Jeff Rollestone, by all that's wonderful!

ROL. (*With affected cheerfulness.*) Changed a bit since the old Harrow days.

GER. Yes; changed indeed!

ROL. I was a bit of a swell, then.

GER. I am very sorry to see you in so sad a plight.

ROL. So am I, believe me! I begin to feel it now. Bah! what does it matter? I'm down on my luck, as many a good fellow has been before me. Bless your heart I'm happy enough—in my way. I take things as they come—when they *do* come, which isn't often. Hang it, man, there's no time like the present. Yesterday was a hundred years ago; to-morrow a hundred years hence. I was born when I woke this morning; I shall die when I sleep to-night. That's my philosophy. I can't be worse off, and when a change does come, it's bound to be for the better. Have a cigar? (*Offering one of two cigars rolled up in a bit of paper.*) Upon my soul they are not bad—Caruncho's Intimidads. It's my only extravagance. (*With a forced laugh.*)

GER. Jeff. Rollestone, don't try to humbug me. This show of indifference is forced, anybody can see that. You're in a bad plight, and you want help.

ROL. I'm right enough. Under a cloud, you know, but that'll blow off. Ha! ha! How's the hunting about here? Stiffish country. (*With an assumption of easy indifference.*)

GER. Come, we were dear old chums at Harrow in the old days. You've helped me out of many a fix; why, hang it, you used to lend me money!

ROL. Yes. I remember. It seems odd, now, don't it? But I don't want help. Harrow is past and gone, and many other good things with it. Let bygones go by. I'm right enough.

GER. You're about as wrong as you can be. You're an educated man, and by rights a man of good position, with claims to associate with none but gentlemen. You have no more right to force yourself into a class so much below you than a tramp would have to associate with men of breeding. It is pitiable to see you in this state ; it is worse than pitiable to hear you express a desire to continue in it.

ROL. (*moved*). Oh, you're right, old fellow, of course. This is as bad as it can be ; but what can I do now ? I get bad fits of memory now and then, and one can't shake off the feelings of a gentleman all at once—they will crop up sometimes ; but still, take it all together, rough and smooth, I——. Oh, damn the thing, let's change the subject.

GER. There was a woman at the bottom of this.

ROL. Yes, don't talk of it.

GER. But if I don't talk of it I don't see how I'm to help you. Come, we're back again at Harrow, by the stile in Johnson's field ; we had no secrets from each other then, let's have none now. Tell me all about it ; was it long since ?

ROL. Yes, ten years.

GER. Where ?

ROL. At Brighton.

GER. Did she treat you badly ?

ROL. No ; it was no fault of hers. I believe she was really fond of me. I was rather a nice-looking boy then, and dressed well ; you wouldn't think that, would you ? I fell in love with her. That may mean that I met her at a ball, danced three times with her, hung about the Pier when the band played, sulked when she flirted, and took my revenge by flirting too. Well, in this case, it don't mean that. It means that in her presence I was subject to an influence that

no magic in the old tales can match. It means that I was changed from a hearty, healthy boy to a pale, trembling, nervous rag. I could scarcely speak in her presence, and I shook like a leaf when I met her. She was only sixteen, but she saw what I suffered, and she took pity on me. I believe she loved me very dearly. At length her people found it out; all Brighton had known it weeks before, and being poor as rats and proud as Lucifer, they forbade me the house. Well, we were finally separated. She fell ill, poor girl, and the doctors, who found out how the land lay, ordered her abroad as her only chance. I mooned about from town to town for a couple of years, when I heard that she was going to be married to a man, I won't trust myself to name even now; and on the wedding day I went mad and drank myself into a red hot fever that lasted six weeks. When I pulled through I went abroad, played at Homburg and Baden, drank,—lost all I had, took to the stage, drank,—wrote for low-class papers, betted, drank,—marked at a billiard saloon, drank,—tramped, drank,—and here I am, fit for nothing better than to sit to my old chum as a model scamp, very much at your service, old man; and after that long yarn I'll take a drink—your good health, Jerry Seaton, and may you pull through better than I have done. (*Drinks from flask.*)

GER. Now the only question is, what's to be done?

ROL. Nothing; I'm too far gone for help.

GER. At least you want money?

ROL. Thanks, I'm not a beggar. I've earned half-a-sovereign—give me that and I'll be off.

GER. You'll not stir from this place until I've made up my mind what's to become of you.

ROL. If there's an opening for a respectable scarecrow that knows his business——

GER. (*suddenly*). By Jove! I wonder if you would——?

ROL. Of course I would. Tell me off to my field, and I'll begin to-day.

GER. Nonsense. My father's secretary and agent has just left him. He asked me this morning to look out for somebody for him. The duties are light, and so's the salary. He's the kindest old man in the world, and he's never so happy as when he's pulling a poor fellow out of the mud. Come. What do you say?

ROL. Do I look like a private secretary?

GER. No, I can't say you do—but you shall. My traps are in O'Hara's cottage, waiting for the cart that is to take them down to the station. I can fit you out in no time.

ROL. No. I can't do it. I am well enough as I am.

GER. Well enough? Think of *her!* of what *she* would say to that. Come. Stop with us a week or so, and try how you like the work; there's not much to do: I'm off to the South to-day, but you'll get on capitally with O'Hara, my father's bailiff. I'll go and look out some clothes for you, and you can follow me when you've made up your mind.

[*Exit* GERARD *into cottage.*

ROL. Aye--what would she think? Oh, my darling, dead and gone to me, but living and loving a better man than I, if ever a thought of poor broken-hearted Jeff Rollestone saddens your gentle mind, think of him only as he was in the days that are gone! The chance that this large-hearted, impulsive, foolish fellow offers me—have I a right to take it? I, idle, dissolute, and a vagabond! How can I, bent with the burden of my shame, hold up my head among the blameless women of a cultured English home? A gentleman again! By

a strange chance a gentleman! Gerard Seton, I take you at your word. The world will call you a fool for placing faith in such as I. I'll prove the world a liar!

[*Exit into cottage.*

As ROLLESTONE *goes off*, MISS PARMINTER *enters cautiously*.

MISS P. The man has gone into the cottage—you can come now, Marion. (*Enter* MARION).

MAR. (*going to the sketch and looking at it*). Ah, that's better—much better. Don't you think so.

MISS P. It is a work of art. Gerard Seton is, indeed, a surprising genius.

MAR. Gerard Seton, a genius? Ha! ha! ha! Don't be angry, Miss Parminter—but you have put my poor humdrum cousin in such an entirely novel light!

MISS P. (*surprised*). Don't you think he's a genius?

MAR. No, indeed, I don't!

MISS P. (*aside*). Hum! Curious; I suppose she don't like geniuses.

MAR. Gerard is much better than a genius. He's a thoroughly good fellow, and I have a very sincere regard for him.

MISS P. (*shaking her hand*). Thank you—thank you. You have simplified my task for me.

MAR. (*surprised*). What task?

MISS P. Marion, that man's wife will be a fortunate woman.

MAR. His wife? Gerard with a wife! There's another point of view from which I never regarded him. But now that you mention it, I think he ought to settle down into a very fair husband, as husbands go. He's not too young, and he's not too good-looking.

MISS P. There I don't agree with you. I think he s extremely handsome – though I own that he is looking very ill just now.

Mar. Ill? I never saw him looking better!

Miss P. No. He has a colour—but it is a hectic flush. His face wears a smile, but it is a sickly smile. His step is springy and elastic—but it is the elasticity of nervous agitation. Oh, Marion—my dear, dear friend —how—how can I most fittingly break to you the news with which my mind is charged?

Mar. (*surprised*). News?

Miss P. Gerard seeks a wife.

Mar. A wife?

Miss P. No mere thoughtless girl—he is too sensible for that. Not a poor wife, but one whose income will supplement the deficiencies of his own. Oh, Marion, cannot you guess—cannot you guess?

Mar. My dear Miss Parminter, you don't mean to say——

Miss P. Yes, Marion, I do, I do. Tell me that you are not angry with him!—tell me that you are not angry with *me!*

Mar. Angry? No! Surprised—very, very much surprised—yes!

Miss P. But you must have remarked his attentions —his affectionate solicitude?

Mar. No, indeed. Gerard is always kind and attentive to everyone—but I have seen nothing in his conduct to prepare me to expect such an announcement from you.

Miss P. And now tell me—what shall I say to him? For I have promised to let him know this very afternoon.

Mar. Do you wish me to speak candidly?

Miss P. Quite candidly and unreservedly.

Mar. You will not be angry?

Miss P. Angry? No! But I shall be very sorry indeed if your reply is unfavourable.

MAR. Then, Miss Parminter, as you want my un
qualified opinion, I will speak quite frankly. My view
of the case is that the difference in age alone should
put anything like an engagement out of the question.

MISS P. There is a difference of only a very few
years.

MAR. Perhaps, but I cannot take your view of the
matter. I know Gerard well, and I know you too, and
believe me, Miss Parminter—there is no disguising it—
you and he are *not* suited to one another.

MISS P. (*bridling up.*) Marion Callendar—if this is a
joke——

MAR. Oh, Miss Parminter, I could not joke on any
matter in which the happiness of so very old a friend is
concerned. And for that very reason I must speak
plainly. You have a good income, and—and (oh, pray
forgive me) you are not in your first youth—he is still a
young man, and he is poor. Ask yourself if it is probable
—I will even say possible—that your married life can
be a happy one?

MISS P. (*with touching dignity*). Marion Callendar,
this is very cruel of you. I don't think I have deserved
this. You are right in saying that I am not in my first
youth, that is only too evident. I am an old maid. I
am candid enough to own that I am very sorry for it.
But a young and attractive woman should, in pity, be
careful how she jests on such a subject. You have
had your laugh at me—but you have wounded me very
sorely—very, very sorely!

[*Exit* MISS PARMINTER.

MAR. Why, what in the world does she mean? She
begged me to be quite candid, and——. Oh, Gerard,
I'm very much ashamed of you. It's too ridiculous—
it's contemptible. Miss Parminter and Gerard? Oh,
it's impossible to treat it seriously! Ha! ha! ha!

Enter GERARD *from cottage.*

GER.   My dear Marion, what are you laughing at ?

MAR.   Gerard, I am very angry with you.

GER.   I'm very sorry to hear that—on this day of all others.

MAR.   What is this nonsense that you've been putting into that poor young thing's head. She actually believes that you are in love with her !

GER.   (*aside.*) She's seen Jessie, and it's all over with me ! (*Aloud.*) My dear Marion, I am very sorry that this has reached your ears ; but believe me it is nothing serious.

MAR.   Come, tell me all about it.

GER.   It began years ago—when she was younger—for you know we are not friends of yesterday.

MAR.   No, you have known her from childhood, and that makes it so much worse.

GER.   When she first left Drumferry she asked me if she might write to me for advice, if any trouble came to her ; and of course I said " Yes "—how could I say no ?—and the letters came ; such innocent letters, Marion, so full of girlish simplicity—(MARION *much amazed*)—and she seemed to take such pleasure in writing to me, that I had not the heart to break off the correspondence. At last I found that the poor little woman cared for me, for in her last letter she told me so. I was very, very sorry, for I would not have injured a hair of her head.

MAR.   (*in blank astonishment.*) The man must be mad !

GER.   I am very sorry—heartily sorry. If I had foreseen the end I would most certainly not have encouraged her to write to me. But there was something so touching in the implicit confidence she placed in me, and I suppose something so flattering to my vanity, that I had not the heart, until to-day, to tell her that

this state of things must come to an end. She is a very fascinating little body, I can tell you.

MAR. Fascinating! Well, there's no accounting for tastes! She is intelligent, and shrewd, and amiable, I admit, but beyond that I am quite at a loss to see where her special attraction lies.

GER. (aside). Astonishing how unfair women are to each other. (Aloud). But, come, let's say no more about it. No harm has been done, and, upon my honour as a gentleman, she is as pure and as spotless as yourself.

MAR. Oh, I've no doubt of that !

GER. It is very unlucky that this little matter should have cropped up to-day, for I cannot help fearing that it may prejudice you against me when it is a matter of vital importance that you should think well of me.

MAR. It was too bad of you to allow her to go so far ; but don't suppose I am seriously angry with you for a form of amusement which I simply cannot understand.

GER. Thank you, Mallie ; thank you, sincerely. You give me courage. Marion, we have always been very close friends, have we not ?

MAR. The best friends in the world. And so we always will be.

GER. I hope so, with all my heart and soul.

MAR. Why, I have always looked upon you as a brother, and so I shall, as long as I live.

GER. No.—not as long as you live.

MAR. (alarmed). Why ? What do you mean ?

GER. Marion, there is a closer love than that—do you think you could give it to me ?

MAR. Oh, Gerard !

GER. Come —think how many years we have known one another—how we have trusted one another in everything. How few men and women start on their married life with so full a knowledge of each other—with so full an assurance that, as far as temper and tastes go, they will most certainly be happy? Come, Marion, tell me that our regard, our affection for one another is not to remain where it is?

Mar. Oh, Gerard—what a pity—what a pity! This unconstrained friendship of ours was so pleasant—so very pleasant. This is not kind—this is not fair.

Ger. I am very unhappy. I believe you cannot love.

Mar. I do not love, but I have loved. Not my poor husband, who, good man, as he was, I could do no more than respect. The love that was in me, I had squandered before I knew him, and when my father urged me to marry him, I was—in love—a bankrupt. Come, dear Gerard, let it remain on the old footing. You are very dear to me, my good cousin, and it would pain me very sorely if I doubted that I was equally dear to you. Come—be satisfied with this—I will marry no one else. Let it be as I have said, at all events, for the present; and kiss me, like a dear old friend.

Ger. So be it, then. (*Sighing—he kisses her forehead*). But I cannot give up all hope so easily. Think over what I have said—think it over, gravely and calmly—and when we meet again, time may have worked a change.

Mar. Perhaps. Who can tell? But in the meantime, promise me this—that you will tell no one of what has passed between us to-day. Not even your father.

Ger. On my honour, I promise. (*He kisses her again as* ROLLESTONE *enters from the cottage. He is dressed like a gentleman, and presents a marked contrast to his appearance in*

the early part of the Act). Mallie, let me present to you a very old and dear friend, who has consented to take my father's secretaryship. Mr. Rollestone, Mrs. Callendar.

[PICTURE—ROLLESTONE *and* MARION *recognise one another, and exhibit signs of suppressed emotion.* MARION *seems likely to faint, as* MISS PARMINTER *enters.*]

GER. Marion, what is the matter?

MISS P. Fetch some water—she is going to faint. (MARION *becomes insensible*). Oh Gerard, Gerard; this is your fault!

END OF ACT I.

32

ACT II.

SCENE. *Library at Drumferry. Evening. Large French windows at angle of scene,* R U E *and* L U E, *giving on to balconies. Door* C. MR. SETON *discovered in evening dress, reading. He is a very old gentleman of pleasant and refined aspect.*

Enter JAKES *with lamps.*

Mr. S. Has Mr. Rollestone returned yet ?.

JAKES. Not yet, sir.

Mr. S. Dear me ; he must have missed his train.

JAKES. The train may be late, sir. There is a fair at Portlock to-day.

MR. S. True. Let me know, the moment he arrives.

JAKES. Yes, sir.   [*Exit* JAKES.

MR. S. This state of suspense is intolerable. Three days, and not so much as a telegram ! If he only knew how much depends upon the success of his mission—but it would never do to let that go out of the family, before the time. Well, if ruin comes, we must face it !—we must face it !

Enter MISS PARMINTER.

MISS P. Mr. Seton, is anything wrong ?

MR. S. No—no. I am anxious about Rollestone ; he brings me grave news—grave news—and he should have been here before this.

33

Miss P. Mr. Seton, you must compose yourself. At the worst, the consequences cannot be really serious.

Mr. S. Clara, I can trust you, and I will tell you the truth. If Rollestone has been unsuccessful in effecting a further mortgage on Drumferry (and I confess I have little faith in his financial abilities), the old place, in which my family has lived and died, through ten generations, must inevitably come to the hammer. I owe £12,000, and I don't know where to turn for £500.

Miss P. This is terrible news, indeed.

Mr. S. Yes, terrible—terrible! My only hope lies with Gerard and Marion. If he marries her, her money will free Drumferry, which I should, of course, settle upon her. They would live here, and I think I could count on them for an asylum in my old age. For, Clara, I am a very old man.

Miss P. Not very old, Mr. Seton.

Mr. S. Ah? (*Pleased*). Well, well—perhaps not very old. We will say not very old. How is Marion after her long journey?

Miss P. Better. She will be down presently.

Mr. S. Poor girl—poor girl. Gerard absolutely refuses to discuss the question, and I can get nothing out of him, except that he has some hope of success. But I am not an acute cross-examiner. (*Pause.*) I say, I am rather a clumsy cross-examiner.

Miss P. Indeed. I think you do yourself an injustice, Mr. Seton. If *you* cannot extract the truth, the Old Bailey itself might despair of doing so.

Mr. S. Ah? (*Pleased.*) Well, well—it may be so—it may be so. But do you think there is any chance for him?

Miss P. I don't know. I did not see her, you

know, between her departure from Drumferry, three months ago, and her return to-day.

Mr. S. But surely, in your correspondence with her you have referred to the matter?

Miss P. Mr. Seton, on the day she left, I did attempt to sound her on the subject. It resulted in a particularly painful scene, to which I would rather not recur. I grieve to say that Marion's sense of humour so far misled her as to induce her to refer to the fact that I am elderly, and—and single.

Mr. S. Ridiculous! You elderly? Why *I'm* not so very old, and you're a girl to me! Why, let me see, you're not fifty.

Miss P. (*hurt*). I am not thirty.

Mr. S. Dear me, you surprise me! Tut! tut! I wish Rollestone would come. He's a good fellow, a right good fellow; but he has no head—no head.

Miss P. I look upon Mr, Rollestone as one of the most delightful companions that good fortune has ever placed in my way. Amiable, handsome, accomplished, a fluent speaker, a rarely gifted artist, full of anecdote, brave, gallant as a knight of old—he is my *beau idéal* of a blameless gentleman in the very highest, noblest, and most perfect sense of that much abused word.

Mr. S. Hallo, Clara!

Miss P. I don't care, Mr. Seton, you may laugh at me if you will, I am accustomed to be laughed at; I hold it to be not only absurd, but downright wicked, to allow a false sense of so-called modesty to blind us to the beauties that a bountiful Nature has set before us for our gratification. Mr. Rollestone is entitled to rank with her very noblest works.

Enter Jakes.

Jakes (*announcing*). Mr. Rollestone!

Mr. S. (*nervously*). At last! at last!

35

Enter ROLLESTONE, *as from a journey.*

ROL.   Good evening, Mr. Seton ; I must apologise for appearing before you in this condition, but Jakes told me that you wanted to see me immediately on my arrival.

MR. S. (*with an affectation of ease*).   Ha! ha!   Jakes's zeal must have prompted him to tell you that, for really there was no immediate hurry.   Have you dined ?

ROL.   Thank you, I dined at Portlock.

MR. S.   Then you will take some supper before we talk over business matters.   No ?   As you please. Well, and what news do you bring me ?

ROL.   I am very very sorry to say that I have not been successful.

MISS P.   Oh, Mr. Rollestone !   (*In great distress.*)

MR. S. (*with assumed indifference*).   Indeed ?   Your journey has been fruitless ?   Well, well, happily it is not of much importance.

ROL.   Here is a letter from Mr. Penrose, your solicitor, which no doubt will explain everything to you.   (*Producing large envelope.*)

MR. S.   Ah !   Oblige me by reading it to me.

ROL.   With pleasure—only he desired me to tell you that it was of a specially confidential character, and intended for your own personal information.

MR. S. (*uncomfortable*).   Indeed ?   Ha ! ha !   For my personal information, eh ?   These lawyers, Mr. Rollestone, carry their professional caution to a length which is a—a—simply amusing.   Ha ! ha ! ha !   But I suppose we must humour them, Mr. Rollestone, I suppose we must humour them !

[*Exit* MR. SETON.

MISS P. (*with sentimental earnestness.*)   Mr. Rollestone, I cannot tell you how glad I am that you are safely home again. I began to be very, very anxious for you. Are you weary?

ROL. Not at all, I assure you. To a man who is used to roughing it, a few hours' run in the Limited Mail is a very small matter. Besides, I had a pleasant companion in O'Hara, who joined the train at Portlock. He has just been placed on the Commission of the Peace, and he can talk of nothing else.

MISS P. Captain O'Hara a magistrate! Mr. Seton is too good-natured.

ROL. Oh! you mustn't abuse O'Hara—he and I are great allies. He has a niece whom he strongly recommends to my notice; and who knows but that some day I may marry into the family.

MISS P. Of that I have no fear. You have had great experience as a traveller, Mr. Rollestone?

ROL. Yes, considerable.

MISS P. Abroad?

ROL. Well, no; principally in England and on foot.

MISS P. On foot? How truly delightful!

ROL. Yes—very pleasant.

MISS P. You see so much more of the country on foot—the cozy old cottages—the pretty peeps through leafy avenues—the quaint old village churches—the weather-worn market crosses—the—the—

ROL. The beadles—the police-stations—the notices about vagrants—the parish unions—and the dogs.

MISS P. Yes, you see those too, of course. Oh, Mr. Rollestone, I could live in the open air—couldn't you?

ROL. Well, I happen to know that I *could*; but I'd rather not.

MISS P. My idea of complete happiness is to pack up a bundle of the merest necessities, and start off, never knowing in the morning where I shall sleep at

night ; taking my chance of what I can get to eat, and putting up with the homely accommodation of a quiet village inn. That, Mr. Rollestone, is my idea of perfect happiness. With an intellectual companion like—like yourself, one would never tire of such a life. Never, oh never ! (*Sentimentally.*)

ROL. (*gravely*). Miss Parminter, will you answer me one question, sincerely, truthfully ?

MISS P. (*much agitated*). Yes, yes ! Oh, certainly ! (*Aside*). What in the world is he going to say ?

ROL. Without the least reserve or the smallest equivocation ?

MISS P. (*earnestly*). I think —yes, I *think* I may promise that. Yes, Jeffery Rollestone, I'm *sure* I can !

ROL. Quite, quite sure ?

MISS P. Quite, quite sure !

ROL. Well, then. Did you ever sleep for a week under a damp haystack ?

MISS P. Good gracious, no !

ROL. Because I have, and I don't recommend it. I have tried it, and it has tried me—tried me very much, and, believe me, it's a mistake. If you want to travel, place your faith in Bradshaw, wire on for your bed, and don't turn up your nose in a Hotel Company, however limited. I know what I am talking about. I have been penniless for days at a time—dinnerless, supperless, bedless. A tramp, Miss Parminter, amusingly miserable, and ridiculously hungry !

MISS P. Poor fellow (*aside*). And all this for no fault of your own, I am sure.

ROL. Oh, I beg your pardon, it was very much my own fault. I allowed a disappointment, that most men would have whistled out of their minds, to sap my energies—to undermine my moral strength. I wanted resolution to make a stand against it. Misfortune a burglar, who is always on the look out to break into you. Keep your bars up, iron-plate your doors, put bells on your shutters, tell the police to keep an eye on him, and you are pretty safe. But if he manages to break in, in spite of precautions, treat him as a burglar should be treated : close with him, floor him, throttle him, if you can ; but don't cry out, " Take my nerves, my heart, my resolution, and my energies, but spare my miserable life !" Because, Miss Parminter, life without those other advantages is not worth having.

Miss P. I wish you could contrive to instil a little of your philosophy into Mr. Seton !

Rol. Now tell me the truth. This news that I bring him is of graver moment than he is willing to admit. Is this not so ?

Miss P. I—I cannot deny it. But he is most anxious that the state of his affairs should not be disclosed until the very latest moment. Mr. Rollestone, he is a ruined man ! Oh, what is to be done ?

Rol. I am not given to gush, and I don't believe in the man who is, but if cutting off my two legs would place Mr. Seton on *his*, he might amputate them to-night.

Miss P. I am sure of it. Your devotion to Mr. Seton and his family is one of the most unaccountable, and, at the same time, one of the most touching circumstances in my experience.

Rol. Miss Parminter, suppose that through misfortune, deserved or otherwise, you had lost every penny you possessed, that your friends had given you up as hopeless, and had fallen away from you one by one, as friends will, until you found yourself absolutely alone in the world—a solitary outcast—with only your sense of shame and the recollection of happier days for your companions—without home, without food, without

even the very barest necessaries of existence. Say that when at your very worst and there seemed nothing for it but to make an end and have done with it, you found an unexpected friend in an all but stranger—a man of influence and social standing—who held out his hand to you to drag you from the slough into which you had fallen, and restore you to the position you had forfeited. What would you do for that man?

Miss P. I would work for him till I dropped.

Rol. Take it, that in addition to all this, in his determination to place you in the way of earning an honourable living, he had even admitted you to the privacy of his own blameless home, and established you there in a confidential position—a dependent, indeed, in name, but in fact a dear and intimate and a trusted friend. What would you do for that man?

Miss P. (*with enthusiasm*). Mr. Rollestone, I would die for him!

Rol. So would I. (*Shaking her hand.*)

Miss P. (*rising—aside*). Poor fellow! How bitterly he has suffered, and how noble is his gratitude to those who have rescued him from his degradation! Oh, Jeffery Rollestone, I know a road that would lead *you*, at least, to a snug home with a comfortable independence; but so artificial is the constitution of the society in which we move, that I am forbidden to point it out to you! [*Exit* Miss Parminter.

Rol. Seton ruined! This is sad news indeed! It is terrible to groan under a weight of obligation and yet to be powerless to help at such a time—terrible to know that when the crash comes one can only stand by and idly wring one's hands with the rest. Why, Seton's collie could do as much to help as I! There's not a hope on earth I'd not forego to be able to lend him a hand at this terrible time!

40

Enter MR. SETON. *He is pale and anxious, but he endeavours to appear unconcerned.*

MR. S. Mr. Rollestone, I--I have read Mr. Penrose's letter. Its contents are serious—certainly serious. I—I am going to place a great trust in you.

RÓL. I am very glad to think I deserve your confidence.

MR. S. Indeed you have been very valuable to me. I appreciate your good and earnest services, I assure you. I confess I don't know what I should have done without an able secretary at such a time, for in all matters of business we Setons are a very muddle-headed race.

ROL. Well, Mr. Seton, if my opinion had been asked, I should have said that they were singularly prescient and clear-headed.

MR. S. *(pleased).* Ah? Well, I may be wrong, we will hope I am. I must admit that in selecting you as my secretary my son has shown remarkable discernment.

ROL. I am sensible only of his and your unbounded kindness.

MR. S. Nonsense. We Setons are a very selfish family. When we do a good action, we have a good, sound, worldly reason for it, depend upon it. Why, even now, I am going to take advantage of this sense of gratitude of yours (most uncalled for I am sure); but my maternal grandfather was in trade, and the retail blood in my veins teaches me never to neglect an opportunity.

ROL. Indeed, Mr. Seton, you do yourself injustice.

MR. S. *(pleased).* Ah? Well, well, perhaps I *am* rather hard on myself. I am glad to think I am. However, to business ; Mr. Rollestone, I am a very poor man, it is useless to disguise it from you, I—I am all but ruined. There is only one hope for us. Gerard is, as

you may be aware, very deeply attached to his cousin.

RoL. To his cousin ?

Mr. S. To Marion Callendar. (ROLLESTONE *much moved*). You did not know this ?

Rol. (*agitated*). No, Mr. Seton, indeed I did *not* know it ! I did not even know that Mr. Callendar was dead.

MR. S. You surprise me. Yes, he died three years since at Florence, and Gerard has been for a long time very much attached to Marion, who, by the way, arrived this afternoon.

RoL. Mrs. Callendar here ! (*In great surprise*).

Mr. S. Yes; on a visit for some weeks. Now, I am extremely anxious that she and Gerard should hit it off. She is a very charming and accomplished woman, and she has what no Seton ever had—money and brains. (*A pause*, ROLLESTONE *is much agitated*). I say the Setons never had any brains at all.

RoL. (*abstractedly*). Yes. I understand.

MR. S. (*disappointed*). Oh ! Now Gerard is unaccountably close about it, and I can't quite make out on what terms they parted. My own impression is that he has proposed to her, and that she has taken time to consider. You see, there is not much to attract her. We are not rich, and as a race we are not handsome— (*pause as before*)—I say as a race we are plain.

RoL. (*pre-occupied*). No doubt.

Mr. S. Deuced plain.

RoL. Yes—yes. I—I have remarked it.

MR. S. (*disappointed*). Oh ! Now, Gerard will be here to-morrow—and you are an old friend of his—and of hers. Come, say a good word for the boy—do what you can for him. You are young ; she will be interested in what you say. I am a dull and uninteresting old dog, and what I say will only bore her. (*Pause as before*). I say I am dull and uninteresting (*pause*), and I shall only bore her.

Rol. (*abstractedly*). No doubt.

Mr. S. (*disappointed*). Oh! Then will you undertake this little bit of diplomacy for me?

Rol. Yes, yes, Mr. Seton, I—I will do my best.

Mr. S. (*rather stiffly*). I have had the good fortune to find you in an acquiescing mood, Mr. Rollestone?

Rol. (*abstractedly*). Yes, I—I am in an acquiescing mood.

Mr. S. (*aside*). D——d acquiescing! [*Exit* Mr. Seton.

Rol. Marion free! And Marion here! Here in this very house! and here to remain for days—for weeks. The old hope of my heart here, and to be the wife of the man who has saved me! And it falls to my lot to plead his cause—to urge upon her every reason why she should forget me, who have cherished her memory for ten long years, and give it to him whose love is but of yesterday. Fortune has played me a sorry trick indeed. Bah! what manner of man am I? I owe a debt—but ten minutes since I was fuming under my inability to discharge it. Now, Jeff Rollestone, here is a chance to test this gratitude of yours. If it is but an empty sound, a high-flown commonplace, court your old love for yourself, and leave these, your stanchest friends—the one heart-broken, the other penniless. No! your course is clear. But there must be no reference to the past, or my resolution will fail me. Bah! what have I to fear? The days of our love are dead and gone, and much has passed since then. Between the child of sixteen and the widow of six-and-twenty there is a wide gulf fixed, and Jeff Rollestone is hardly the man to bridge it over. No! we must meet as though the past had died out of my heart, as it died out of hers—in mercy to her—aye, and in mercy to me.

43

Enter MARION.

MAR. Mr. Seton ; are you here ? (*Sees* ROLLESTONE).
Mr. Rollestone !

ROL. (*confused*). Mrs. Callendar. I——

MAR. Come, Jeffery. Don't let us meet like this.
You must not call me Mrs. Callendar. My name is
still Marion. In that, at least, I am not changed.

ROL. (*with assumed ease.*) Then, Marion, I am very
glad to meet you. I did not know, until a few minutes
since, that you were at Drumferry.

MAR. I arrived a few hours ago. (*Pause*). Jeffery,
we parted under very painful circumstances, and I
have much to say to you. Much that has been on my
mind for many years. But I am a foolish woman, and
I don't know how to begin.

ROL. And I, too, have something to say, and it will
put us both at our ease if I say it first. When we
parted, I thought myself a broken-hearted man, and I
believe I gave you a great deal of unnecessary pain. I
hope you have forgiven me.

MAR. Forgiven you ? What had I to forgive ?

ROL. Now, Marion, let us come to a cozy understanding. You and I were fond of one another as boy
and girl—I believe we told each other as much—but
your mother interfered, and from her point of view, she
was quite right. You went your way, I went mine,
and there was an end of the matter. So there let the
matter end. It—it is strange how quickly we forget
these things.

MAR. (*surprised and pained*). Then things are soon forgotten !

ROL. Yes. Well, now we are much older (at least,
I am, I won't answer for you), and we see this in its
true light. We see how perfectly right your mother

was to separate us—we see that now, don't we? (*Pause*). I say, now that the scratch is healed—the scratch that we inexperienced young people mistook for a gash—now that that has healed over, and we've forgotten all about it, we see how right, how very right your mother was to separate us.

MAR. (*bitterly*). Yes, we see that now!

ROL. Because we really did not know each other.

MAR. No, we did not know each other!

ROL. Then let us be very good friends indeed—very excellent friends—and let us agree that this friendship is so very pleasant and satisfactory in every way that we wouldn't change it for anything else on any account. Shall we settle it so?

MAR. (*sighing*). Yes, we will always be very good friends.

ROL. That's well. It is very kind of you, very kind indeed.

MAR. I had no idea, when we last met, that you knew Mr. Seton.

ROL. I did not know him then, but I knew his son. I knew Gerard.

MAR. Indeed?

ROL. Yes. He and I were at Harrow together, and very close and dear friends. I am very sincerely attached to Gerard. I was a very poor man when he gave me his father's secretaryship.

MAR. I knew that you were poor.

ROL. Yes, your mother made that quite clear to you. (*Hurriedly*) She was right, quite right; but I refer to a condition compared with which my poverty was affluence. I was all but starving!

MAR. Gerard has a very kind and generous heart.

ROL. (*earnestly*). Thank you, Marion, thank you very heartily (*taking her hand*). You have given me great

pleasure. I—I am, of course, deeply interested in the happiness of a man to whom I owe so much.

MAR. No doubt. It is but natural and right that you should be grateful to him. (*With some hesitation.*) Gerard is an intimate friend of yours; has he—has he spoken to you of me?

ROL. No. But his father has told me that Gerard loves you very dearly. Indeed, I believe that Gerard himself has told you as much.

MAR. He has.

ROL. Now—come, Marion—be frank with me— with what result?

MAR. With no result.

ROL. With no result as yet?

MAR. With no possibility of result.

ROL. I am deeply grieved to hear this. Is there no hope for him?

MAR. You are, no doubt, much attached to your friend?

ROL. Very much attached.

MAR. (*bitterly*). I am sorry to say what will evidently give you very deep pain; but—there is no hope.

ROL. None?

MAR. None.

ROL. Come, Marion, don't be angry with me; but *I* am not going to let the matter drop so easily. I take the very deepest interest in the future of both of you —more, perhaps, in your own future than you are disposed to believe.

MAR. (*bitterly*). It may well be so!

ROL. Then bear with me, if, in the interests of you both, I urge you to think of the very best points in his character, and to make the most of them. He is still young—he is a right good fellow, and he bears an old and honoured name. He is not a rich man; but you are rich. You have known him all his life—you and he have been as brother and sister. Think how well you know him, and how comparatively little you can know of another man. All these things plead for him. Come, Marion, by our old regard for each other, think kindly of him as he deserves.

MAR. (*coldly*). Gerard Seton has an eloquent advocate!

ROL. (*warmly*). Gerard Seton has an enthusiastic advocate, and one who hopes in his heart that you can give him hope. Forgive me, Marion, if I have said too much.

MAR. Mr. Rollestone, I am pained and hurt by what you have said, to a degree that scarcely leaves me mistress of my words. It is hard and cruel of you to say these things to me!

ROL. (*surprised*). Hard and cruel?

MAR. Yes. If the old time be dead and gone, so let it be. Let it never be referred to between us. I have no desire to dwell upon it. But I do not like this championship of a man who wishes to marry me, to come from you. It may be vanity, pique—call it what you will—but it is galling to hear you, who once professed a regard for me, advocating the cause of a man who, but for the deadening lapse of time, you would have regarded as a detested interloper. I am a woman, Mr. Rollestone. and this hurts me,

ROL. Marion, for God's sake, let the old time go by.

MAR. With all my heart. It is not pleasant to remember. I was a simple, foolish child when you told me that you loved me, and (*contemptuously*) I believed you!

ROL. I spoke in good faith. I deserved to be believed.

MAR. Perhaps. But see what a wrong you would

have done me. See what a life-blight you would have brought upon me —you, loving and tender for a year, I, loving and tender for a life !

ROL. Indeed, Marion, you do me an injustice. I did not forget so readily. But Gerard Seton——.

MAR. Do not speak to me of Gerard Seton. I have refused Gerard Seton because there is but one man on earth whom I would not refuse, and Gerard Seton is not that man. Let that suffice. I will hear no more on that subject. Gerard and I are very good cousins, and very good cousins we will remain.

ROL. Marion, you try me sorely. I am a careless, idle, irresolute man, and by an effort which is strange to me, I have nerved myself to speak to you on this subject. It has cost me much, and thus I am repaid· It is not just.

MAR. Is it just to me to force me to say unwomanly things to you? Is it right that you should so goad me to forgetfulness of myself, and remembrance of none but you, that I have no resource but to tell you that I am fool enough to love you as in the time that is gone· There, the words are out. I am a headstrong woman. I cannot carry out a plan that involves smooth speaking. I cannot put my words into masquerade. You have brought this avowal on yourself; make the best or the worst of it. Pity me or ridicule me, whichever you will, but for God's sake, if you come to me at all, do not come with another man's name in your mouth. Speak to me of yourself, or be silent.

ROL. If I am not mistaken, you gave him some hope.

MAR. I gave him no hope. I told him that it could never be. You cannot know the pain you have given me. Many years ago you told me that you loved me, and I believed you. To-day you tell me that you did

not love me, and I do not believe you. I will not
believe that the passionate utterance of those days
was a lie—that the mad despair when my parents
took me away from you was a triumph of aimless
hypocrisy. I will not believe that the long-drawn
misery which was known to all who knew you, long
after we had parted, was but the sequel of an elaborate
scheme of objectless deception. Tell me, am I right
in disbelieving this?

Rol.. How can I answer you? What can I say but
that as I seemed to love, so indeed I did love? What
can I say but that as I loved then so do I love now,
and so shall I love to the end!

Mar. (*incredulously*). To the end?

Rol. (*passionately*). Yes, to the end! For I have
fought with this love, and I have found that it is in-
vincible—I have wrestled with it, and I have found
that it is irresistible—I have sought to kill it, and I
have found that it is eternal! I have loved you, and I
have loved no other woman, as I hope to live.

Mar. (*bitterly*). I can believe that this love of yours
is of hardy growth, for it would seem that it can co-
exist with a desire that I should marry your friend. I
compliment you on its vitality.

Rol. I have borne so much for its sake that I can
bear your bitter words now. I pleaded for my friend
because I had promised—because I held it to be my
duty to do so. For myself I took no thought, for I
had no hope. You have kindled a dead hope into life ;
and, duty or no duty, I have words but for myself. In
my weakness, I yielded to my love, in my strength, I
still yield to it! Idly loving you—living but for that
love—living on that love—when it was taken from me,
I yielded up all that was true and manly, and earnest
in my nature. When it went, the best that was in me,

went with it. I became hopeless, soulless, and degraded. Marion, forgive me for the deceit I practised on you, for the love of you is my very breath—the only flower in the tangled weed-grown garden of my misdirected life! (*They embrace.*)

MAR. Jeffery, we will be happy now; there is none between us. I am rich, and mistress of myself. I only live to repair the wrong I did you. No one can part us now; oh, my love!

ROL. No one can part us, now! I have love for none but you.

MAR. (*rising and going to door*). Jeffery, for the life that I am to lead—for the new-found hope of life, I thank you. Dear Jeffery, from my soul, I thank you! Oh, Jeffery, I have been so unhappy—I have been so unhappy! My life has been a lie, and I have wearied under it—but the sun rises on it now, and the past ten years are gone as a tale that is told!

[*Exit* MARION.

ROL. At last! at last! Shall I wake from this, I wonder, and find myself back in my vagabond life—an idle, ill-conditioned, aimless waif! It might well be: many a time when at my worst, I've dreamt such dreams as this—and woke to find myself shivering under a haystack! It cannot be true—It cannot be true!

Enter MR. SETON.

ROLLESTONE *shows agitation at his entrance.* MR. SETON'S *manner is hurried and anxious.*

MR. S. Rollestone, you have seen Marion? You have spoken to her of Gerard? Is it not so?

ROL. It is so.

MR. S. Well—well—and what does she say? Eh? Rollestone, every hope I have in the world is centred

D

on her and on him. She—she spoke kindly of him, did she not?

Rol. Yes.

Mr. S. I knew it—I was sure of that. Well, tell me—tell me. I want to know the best and the worst.

Rol. Mr. Seton, be patient with me. I have a difficult task to discharge.

Mr. S. Patient! Mr. Rollestone, you cannot know how I am situated, or you would see the irony of your request. I implore you to tell me, without delay or equivocation, what took place between you.

Rol. I spoke of your son—I urged every argument—but, although she has a sincere regard for him—a very deep and sincere regard for him—that is all.

Mr. S. Good God, Mr. Rollestone, then we are lost—utterly ruined and undone—and the old place, with all that is in it, must go to the hammer! Oh, Mr. Rollestone, you are not playing with me?

Rol. You cannot suppose that I should speak otherwise than earnestly in a matter in which your prosperity and his happiness are so nearly concerned.

Mr. S. No—no. I do not suppose that—but I met her as she left you—she was crying—but she told me that she was very happy. I find it difficult to reconcile that with a deliberate and hopeless rejection of an old and valued friend.

Rol. I must beg your forgiveness for what I am going to tell you. I loved your niece, many years ago.

Mr. S. *(in great surprise)*. Mr. Rollestone!

Rol. When we met, I endeavoured to stifle that love, for your sake and for his; I so far succeeded as to bring myself to urge Gerard's claim upon her with the earnestness of an advocate whose heart is in his cause. She told me that it was useless. She then told me, to

my unspeakable surprise, that her old love for me was yet alive.

MR. S. (*trembling with rage.*) Mr. Rollestone, I am utterly at a loss to express my astonishment, my amazement, my indignation at your statement, I—I placed a confidence in you, and you have betrayed it ; I trusted you, and you have forsaken your trust.

ROL. Mr. Seton, I have told you what took place, in the fewest possible words. If I were to explain myself at length, I think you would judge me more fairly. (*going*).

MR. S. Stop sir. Rollestone, don't let us part like this—I have been kind to you ; Gerard has been kind to you—have we not ?

ROL. I am free to confess that I owe you a debt of gratitude I can never hope to repay.

MR. S. Wrong, wrong, my dear boy—you can repay it now — you can repay it twenty-fold ! I am not accustomed to refer to benefits I may have conferred; if I do so now, it is under the pressure of the most urgent necessity ; you say you owe me a debt—you do ! you wish to repay it—you can ! Rollestone, this union was in a fair way of accomplishment, when he and I rescued you from your forlorn and pitiable condition. Is that act of kindness to prove our ruin ? And is it fit that you, of all men, should be the instrument by which our ruin is to be worked ? Come, Rollestone, ask yourself this, and we are saved.

ROL. (*agitated*). Mr. Seton, you ask much of me—too much ! The debt I owe you is a heavy one indeed, but, after all, it is finite, and the price you would have me pay is infinite. Marion Callendar has given me her love ; it is a sacred and solemn trust, and I may not go from it.

Mr. SETON (*passionately*). Then, sir, I have only one

word to say : Leave my house at once—at once ! I
have shown you a kindness which should have ensured
the gratitude of the veriest reprobate. It has failed to
ensure yours. Go, sir, you have ruined us. I hope I
shall never see you or hear of you again.

Exit MR. SETON *trembling with passion. During this speech
the light of the moderator lamp has died out, and the moonlight through* R. C. *window supplies the only light on the
stage.*

ROL. So the end is at hand ! What am I to do.
My duty. Aye, but duty is a tool that, from long dis-
use, I handle clumsily, and who knows against whom I
may turn it ? Marion has given me her love—have I
a right to forego it ? Have I a right to say to her,
" There is none who needs your love as I need it, but
there are those to whom your wealth is life and death,
take your money to them, and with it the love that
I have hungered for these ten long years " ? No !
And yet Gerard loves her—he is a right good fellow—he
should make her a true and worthy husband, and he
has saved *me !* Yes, he has saved me, and I repay his
good deed by robbing him of the woman who, but for
that deed, would have married him. There is only one
thing certain, I must leave Drumferry to-night. Seton
has made that clear enough, and once away from this,
a cool head and a quiet pulse may help me to see my
way to the right thing to do !

During these lines ROLLESTONE *has sauntered to the balcony
(*R U E). *As he finishes this speech he sees the window lead-
ing to the balcony (*L U E) *slowly and cautiously open. He
stands by, watching attentively, as* QUILT *slowly enters
through the window, looking stealthily about him.*

QUILT. So far so good—every light in the house is
out, there's not so much as a black-beetle stirring ! Ah,

everything is as it used to be in the old time! Its a touching thing to come upon it again, and like this, too! And there's the bureau in which that devil keeps his letters—curse him (*tries it*)! Locked! Ah, he never locked it when *I* was his father's secretary! No, no— he trusted *me*! It must be a pleasant reflection to my successor to know that I was trusted, and he isn't. I shall have to fall back on these—(*producing skeleton keys*), though I don't know much about using them, and I don't like to ask. It's a delicate question to ask! (*proceeds to pick lock*—ROLLESTONE *takes a chair, unseen by him, and watches his proceedings*). That wont do—stop a bit—I've got it now—There! (*desk open*) What's this? Unpaid bills? (*taking out a huge file filled with papers*), and what's this—Receipts (*takes out a small file with two or three papers on it*). There's a dishonest vagabond! Hallo! here are the letters, sure enough—just where he always leaves them. (*takes one and opens it—reads*) " My darling—" yes, damn him, that's right enough! *reading letter with his back towards* ROLLESTONE. " My darling," she never said half as much to me!

ROL. I beg your pardon—are you looking for any-thing?

QUILT. Who's there? (*much alarmed and startled— crams the letter he was reading into his trousers pocket*).

ROL. The very question I was going to ask you.

QUILT (*assuming an air of recklessness*). Now, look here—I am not going to be trifled with.

ROL. You are quite right—you are *not* going to be trifled with. (*Produces a pipe case, which closes with a loud snap. He holds it as if it were a pistol—which, indeed,* QUILT *takes it for.*) On the contrary, if it is any satis-faction to you to know it, you are going to be treated very seriously, indeed.

QUILT. How, sir? (*Much alarmed.*) There's no occasion to use a pistol. I'm not a common burglar—I'm a man of honour—though I admit my presence here, at this hour, does seem to call for some explanation.

Rol. Well, at the first blush, there is an indistinct-ness—a want of context, if I may so express myself—in your presenting yourself in Mr. Seton's library at this hour, which makes it difficult to grasp the full value of the situation.

Quilt. I see what you mean.

Rol. Thank you. You see—when I find a stranger breaking open my employer's desk at midnight, why that is an isolated fact which (primâ facie) does seem, as you say, to want explanation. In fact, I don't see how we are to get on without it.

Quilt. Mr. Rollestone, I will be quite frank with you.

Rol. Do Fire away—if you don't, I shall.

Quilt. I am Mr. Richard Quilt, Mr. Seton's late secretary.

Rol. Oh. Didn't you understand that you were discharged ?

Quilt. Yes, yes. Mr. Seton made that quite clear.

Rol. Then to what shall we attribute your presence in his library to-night ? Shall we say force of habit ?

Quilt. Mr. Rollestone, between a discharged secre-tary and his successor there should be no secrets. There is a young lady at the bottom of this—a young lady to whom I am sincerely and devotedly attached. That young lady has listened to the malignant overtures of a gilded snake.

Rol. As women will !

Quilt. Exactly. Now, do you know the name and address of that snake ? Gerard Seton of Drumferry !

Rol. What !

Quilt. Gerard Seton. He has beguiled her into a correspondence—he has a dozen and more of her let-

ters—and the villain threatens to publish them, unless she listens to him, and throws me over. What do you say to that?

ROL. I say that it's a lie.

QUILT. A lie? Look here! One, two, three, four —sixteen of 'em. I've waited for weeks for an opportunity of getting at them, but the windows have always been fastened, and my chance didn't come till to-night.

ROL. I don't think much of it now that it *has* come.

QUILT. Don't judge me harshly. If you have ever loved a girl with all your heart, and you had a rival, you'd do any dirty thing to gain her. Wouldn't you, now? Come—as a gentleman, wouldn't you?

ROL. No—I think not. (*Pause.*) Now attend to me, and if you move right or left, you're a dead man. (*Pointing the pipe case at* QUILT). Throw me that bundle of letters.

QUILT. No, no, Mr. Rollestone, you're asking too much.

ROL. I'm not asking more than I intend to enforce (*pointing the pipe case at him*). Throw me those letters.

QUILT. You're a nice kind of secretary to go about with a loaded pistol in your pocket! There, damn you! (*Throws him the bundle of letters*).

ROL. (*aside—contemplating them*). Oh, Gerard, Gerard, I'm sorry for this!

QUILT (*eagerly*). Read them, read them, you'll see that I've spoken the truth.

ROL. Thank you, but they are not addressed to me (*puts them into his pocket*).

QUILT. Now—what are you going to do to me?

ROL. I will show you (*pointing pipe case at him*). In the first place empty your pockets.

(QUILT *empties his coat pockets*).

ROL. Call out the articles, one by one.

56

QUILT. A pocket-handkerchief.

ROL. Yours. You may keep it.

QUILT. A piece of rope.

ROL. Mine. Throw it here. (QUILT *throws it to* ROLLESTONE).

QUILT. A complete angler.

ROL. Yours. I don't fish.

QUILT. A box of live bait.

ROL. Yours.

QUILT (*producing a heavy life preserver*). A light cane.

ROL. Mine. Throw it here. (QUILT, *furious, is about to hurl it*). Not too hard. (QUILT *tosses it to him with a muttered oath*). Thank you.

QUILT. That's all.

ROL. Very good. Now take off your coat.

QUILT. Come, come; a gentleman's wardrobe is sacred.

ROL. I think you'd better. (QUILT *takes it off, and throws it to him.*) Now your waistcoat. (*He does as directed.*) Now take off that pair of ——

QUILT. What, sir?

ROL. Don't be alarmed—boots. Now, turn your back to me, and put your hands behind you. (QUILT *does so.* ROLLESTONE *makes a " clove-hitch " in the cord, and puts it over* QUILT's *wrists—securing them*). There.

QUILT. You devil!

ROL. Not at all. This strap is for your ancles. (*He straps* QUILT's *ancles.*) There! now you're harmless.

QUILT. Are you going to give me into custody?

ROL. I don't know. I'm going to think you out. (*Sits smoking, and contemplating* QUILT, *who stands uncomfortably*). Now shall I detain you, or shall I let you go?

QUILT (*eagerly*). If you detain me, all about those letters is bound to come out.

ROL. True.

57

QUILT. Gerard Seton will lose his chance with the heiress.

ROL. No doubt.

QUILT. The young girl who wrote these letters—her character will be gone for ever.

ROL. Your arguments are convincing. You may go.

QUILT (*surprised*). Scot free?

ROL. Scot free.

QUILT. Come, that's handsome.

ROL. No thanks ; you can go.

QUILT. I'm sorry I spoke roughly.

ROL. Don't mention it. *I* should have been annoyed if it had happened to me. (*Pause.*) Well, why don't you go?

QUILT. What! tied up like this ?

ROL. Yes—tied up like that !

QUILT. But, hang it, I can only hop !

ROL. Then, hang it, hop away !

QUILT. But anyone who sees me in this condition is certain to detain me.

ROL. No doubt. That's exactly what I want. You see I'm in rather a delicate position. If I give you into custody, Mr. Gerard Seton's share in this matter (whatever it is) would certainly be made public, and he might not like that. By letting you go as you are, you will certainly be arrested by one of the keepers ; you will be brought before Mr. Seton or his son (who will be here to-morrow), and he can either prosecute you on the more serious charge or release you altogether—as he thinks fit.

QUILT (*in a rage*). You cursed villain ! But for the accident of your being armed with a pistol, I'd have beaten your brains out before I'd have surrendered those letters !

ROL. Ha ! ha ! no doubt ! But you must never

expect to find me unprepared. (*Opening pipe case and taking out pipe.*) This deadly weapon and I are inseparable.

QUILT. Done! But I'll be even with you for this! If I come well out of this fix, before I'm a week older I'll batten on your very heart's blood! (*He speaks these words melodramatically, then turns round short, hops to the window, and so off*).

ROL. (*watching him from window.*) Poor devil! There he goes across the lawn. Hallo! he's down—now he's up again! He looks perfectly spectral in the moonlight! Now, Gerard Seton, is this fellow's story true? Here are the letters sure enough, and in a girl's writing; but I have only his word for what they contain. For aught I know they may be quite harmless, and admit of ready explanation. They may relate to a matter that is dead and gone; yet, if they come out, there is an end of all hope for you. One thing, and only one, is quite clear. Whatever these letters may contain, they came into my possession by an accident and in my confidential position in his establishment, and it is my duty to place them in his hands, and in no other's. (*Proceeds to seal them up in an envelope.*)

Enter MR. SETON, *still in evening dress,* MARION *and* MISS PARMINTER *in peignoires.*

MAR. Oh! Mr. Rollestone, we have been terribly frightened!

ROL. Mrs. Callendar, what is the matter?

Miss P. The man—the man!

ROL. What man?

MR. S. I saw from my window a white figure hopping across the lawn in the moonlight. It seemed so extraordinary and unaccountable that we came to ask you if you knew anything at all about it?

ROL. A white figure hopping across the lawn? Very extraordinary!

Miss P. Ghostly, Mr. Rollestone —simply ghostly ! I cannot tell you how appalling it was ! Mr. Rollestone, it was no thing of earth !

Rol. I'll make inquiries at once.

Mr. S. The room is in strange confusion.

Rol. Yes ; I—I have been preparing for a journey (*folding up* Quilt's *coat and waistcoat*). Pray compose yourselves. I will make inquiries at once. At all events if the man has gone there is no occasion for any further alarm.

Mr. S. Come. Miss Parminter, we are safe for the present. (*Going.*)

Rol. (*aside*). Well out of that, at all events.

Enter Captain O'Hara *in great excitement, followed by servants.*

O'H. Stop, stop—Mr. Seton—Mrs. Callendar. I beg your pardon ; but as I was leaving your house just now to go home, Watson, your keeper, found a man, tied hand and foot, endeavouring to climb over the park fence. Watson stopped him, and dragged him into the lodge. He turned out to be Richard Quilt.

Mr. S. Quilt ! My late secretary !

O'H. Yes, that's the man. They asked him what he was doing in the grounds at that time o' night, and as he couldn't give a satisfactory account of himself, they searched him ; and, oh, Mr. Seton—I'm well-nigh heartbroken—for they found on him a letter from my bird—my Jessie !

Miss P. He has often told me that he admired your niece.

O'H. Aye ! But although the letter was found *on* him, it wasn't written *to* him. She despises him, as any girl would ; and the letter is as fond as it can be ! Mr. Seton, I want to know who that letter was wrote to.

Mar. Are you sure of the writing ?

O'H. Sure? Why, how can I doubt it? Lookee here, it's signed by her, and it speaks of me; and as to her writing, didn't I teach her to write? Look at it—read it!

MAR. *(takes the letter and reads it).* " My dear, dear friend."

O'H. Tell me that's addressed to that skulking ape, Quilt?

MAR. *(reading).* " Why have you not written to me? Sometimes I think that my letters only tease you, and then the world might be in ashes for anything I care; but when I see you, you are so kind and gentle with me, that I want to write again and tell you everything that is in my heart.—Your loving, little friend, JESSIE."

O'H. Mr. Seton, I'm a rough customer—I ha'n't got my words rightly under control when my blood's up—and it's up now. There's none hereaway that my poor lass could care about except that smooth-faced son of yours; and, mark this, as sure as I'm a man with two fists, I'll break his damned neck for him.

[MR. SETON *sinks into a chair and covers his face.*

MAR. Captain O'Hara, you have my sincerest sympathy. The world looks lightly on such deeds. I do not go with the world. Mr. Seton, your son and I are very old and dear friends; but if he is guilty of this act, I will never speak to him again!

MR. S. Stop, Marion, stop!—there is no proof—we may be mistaken.

MAR. To whom else in this neighbourhood can this letter have been addressed?

ROL. *(coming forward).* Mrs. Callendar, that letter was addressed to me.

(MARION *horrified,* CAPTAIN O'HARA *furious.* MR. SETON *takes* ROLLESTONE'S *hand gratefully as the Act Drop falls.*)

END OF ACT II.

61

ACT III.

SCENE. *A comfortably furnished, old-fashioned sitting-room in* O'HARA'S *cottage, arranged for examination of* QUILT. *A Windsor chair* L, *a comfortable easy-chair* R C, *facing Windsor chair. A small writing-table with writing materials in front of easy-chair. Other seats about the room for witnesses, &c. A small occasional table near* R *of easy-chair.* DAVID (O'HARA'S *gardener*) *discovered arranging the scene as described. To him enters* O'HARA, *dressed in his best, and rather important in manner.*

O'H. Well, David, is the court o' justice rigged?

DAV. Aye, Cap'en, as far as I can judge. I've arranged it just as you told me. There's a table and an easy-chair for your worship, them seats is for the witnesses and general public, and that 'ere Windsor chair is for the prisoner at the bar, poor chap.

O'H. A Windsor chair for Mr. Quilt? No, no, David, that won't do—not in *my* house. The laws of hospitality must be respected, and no one shall ever say of Dick O'Hara that he took an easy-chair for himself and told off a Windsor for a visitor.

DAV. True, sir; but I thought as Mr. Quilt is in custody——

O'H. Custody? What's that got to do with it? By the law of the land every man is presumed to be innocent till he's proved to be guilty. I won't allow Dick Quilt to be treated like a felon in *my* house, not before he's proved to *be* a felon. Dick Quilt's in a very grave position, and I daresay he's anxious, poor chap. And when you're anxious you want to be comfortable. An anxious chap can't be easy on a Windsor. No, no. Place my table over there. Dick Quilt shall have the easy chair.

(DAVID *moves the table so that it stands in front of the Windsor chair, leaving the arm-chair for* QUILT.)

O'H. That's better—it looks more friendly. Pooh! I wish this was all over!

DAV. So does he, poor chap, I'll go bail! Don't be hard on him, your worshup. A misfortun' like this might happen to any of us—besides, Mr. Quilt and you was very good friends.

O'H. Yes, I always stood up for Dick Quilt. But as a magistrate I've my dooty to do, and I can't allow private friendship to interfere with the course o' justice. Put that decanter near Mr. Quilt's chair, so that he can help himself, David. (DAVID *puts a decanter of sherry and a glass on small table,* R. *of easy chair.*)

DAV. Ah, it's a grand thing to be a magistrate, your worship.

O'H. So it is, David, when so be as you can work a day's reckoning.

DAV. I hope you won't make a fool of yourself, Cap'en. Some beaks do.

O'H. I'm not afraid o' that. There's a very good rule when you've got to deal with a point of law. Hear what both sides have to say, weigh the evidence carefully, come to your own conclusion, and the reverse of that will be the law of the case. Besides, Mr. Seton sent down to say that he shall be present at the examination, and *he'll* set me right if I steer out o' my course. So there's no fear of my going very far wrong, David.

63

Enter Miss Parminter.

Miss P.   Good morning, Captain O'Hara.

O'H.   Your sarvant, ma'am.   Proud and honoured
to have your company on this melancholy occasion,
ma'am.   Your face is welcome as the flowers in May.

Miss P.   Thank you.   (*Aside.*)   He is really much
improved.   His manner is quite Grandisonian.   (*Aloud.*)
Mr. Seton, understanding that I should be present as
a witness, requested me to tell you that he is extremely
unwell this morning, and will be quite unable to be
present at the prisoner's examination.

O'H. (*aghast*).   But, ma'am, you don't mean to tell
me that I've got to work this affair on a dead-
reckoning ?

Miss P.   I am not conversant with legal terms, but
I think it is more than likely.   Mr. Seton regrets very
much——

O'H.   Regrets very much !   But, look here, ma'am,
I don't know anything about it !   I only got my commission as J.P. two days ago, and I never saw a beak
—I should say a magistrate—sitting, since I was bound
'prentice.

Miss P.   Mr. Seton desired me to add that as Mr.
Rollestone, who is quite familiar with the course of
procedure, will be present as a witness, he will no
doubt afford you any assistance of which you may
stand in need.

O'H. (*passionately*).   Mr. Rollestone !   I don't recommend Mr. Rollestone to show his face in *my* house,
after the way he's treated my niece.   I won't have Mr.
Rollestone here, ma'am.   He's a scoundrel, ma'am, a
designing scoundrel !

Miss P.   Believe me, Captain O'Hara, I fully sym-
pathise with your indignation.   He is indeed a bold,

bad man. Yet as he is a principal witness against the prisoner——

O'H. I don't care. I won't have that man here. He excites me. I couldn't administer justice in his presence. I will *not* allow private prejudice to stand in the way of my dooty as a Justice of the Peace. (*To* DAVID.) Are we ready to begin ?

DAV. Quite ready, your worship.

O'H. Then ask the prisoner if he'll be so good as to step this way. I'll work this here matter alone.

DAVID *goes to door* R., *opens it, and* QUILT *enters in custody of a keeper, and followed by two or three servants from Drumferry. He is placed standing in front of easy chair.*

QUILT. This is an unfortunate business, Captain O'Hara.

O'H. Prisoner at the bar, I'm extremely sorry to see a young man of your apparent respectability in so disgraceful a situation. How are you, Dick? (*Shaking his hand.*) Sit down. (QUILT *sits in easy-chair and makes himself comfortable.* O'HARA *goes to his seat on Windsor chair behind table.*) Now, Dick Quilt—I mean prisoner at the bar—you are charged with having burglariously entered the mansion house of Drumferry, and therein maliciously, and, at the prompting of the devil, committing a burglary. Now, prisoner at the bar, there is no nonsense about this court. This court is not particularly well acquainted with its duties, having only received its commission as a magistrate two days ago. You and I, prisoner at the bar, have always been deuced good friends, and as you know a good deal more about these matters than we do, we shall take it as a personal favour if you'll just pull us up whenever you see us steering out of our course.

QUILT. I'm sure I shall be happy to do anything to assist you, Capt. O'Hara.

O'H. Thank you, Dick, I was sure of it, and if you and I don't manage, between us, to get at the rights of this matter, why the deuce is on it. Take a glass of sherry, Dick. Now then—what is the first thing this court does, eh, Dick?

QUILT. Well, if it was me, I should discharge the prisoner.

O'H. Ah, but it ain't you, you know, is it? Come now—no larks, Dick—help us out of this, there's a good chap. (To Miss PARMINTER), let's see, ma'am—the first thing he does is to plead, isn't it?

Miss P. I think it is extremely likely, Capt. O'Hara.

O'H. That is your view?

Miss P. That is certainly my view. But I won't be sure.

O'H. That is quite enough ma'am. A lady's word is law—and law is what we're here for. The first thing you do, Dick—I mean prisoner at the bar—is to plead guilty.

QUILT. But I plead not guilty.

O'H. Oh, I beg your pardon—you plead guilty.

QUILT. I beg yours, Capt. O'Hara—I plead not guilty.

O'H. Well, there you go, you see. If you're going to invent difficulties and obstructions to the course of justice, what's the use of your coming up here in custody?

GUILT. I shall be happy to help you when I can, but I must have an eye to my own interests.

O'H. Very well, then there's an end of the matter. If you'd stood by me and pleaded guilty, I'd have got you off, somehow, but as you plead not guilty, hang me if I don't convict you.

QUILT. I never told a lie yet, and I'm not going to begin now.

F.

O'H. Very well, have it your own way—only let me tell you this—*you've* got me into this fix, and *you'll* have to get me out of it. What's to be done now ?

QUILT. Why call the evidence to be sure.

O'H. Evidence ? What evidence ?

QUILT. Why, evidence that I was seen committing a burglary.

O'H. Well, who saw you commit it ?

QUILT. Oh, I'm not bound to give evidence against myself.

O'H. Bound ! Well, no you're not *bound*, but you and the court have always been good friends, and there should be no secrets between magistrate and prisoner, and—lookee here, Dick Quilt—who saw you do it ?

QUILT. I'm not going to criminate myself.

O'H. (*angrily.*) I don't ask you to criminate yourself. I only ask you, who saw you commit a burglary? Surely, as a friend you can tell me that.

QUILT. Why nobody saw me.

O'H. (*throwing down his pen resignedly.*) Oh, very well. if you won't assist the court, I don't see how we're to get on. Upon my soul, I don't ! The case is adjourned.

They move towards door. Enter ROLLESTONE.

ROL. Stop.

O'H. Hallo, sir, how dare you show your face in my house ?

ROL. I have evidence to give against this man.

O'H. I won't hear it, sir. You—you are an infernal scoundrel. You're a disgrace to humanity.

MISS P. Mr. Rollestone, if you have come here to find out whether Capt. O'Hara has any more lambkins in his fold you have taken needless trouble. Captain O'Hara had but one. [*Exit* MISS PARMINTER.

ROL. Pray reassure yourself—I have come for no

lambkins. I am here to give evidence that will convict this man without fail.

O'H. I tell you, sir, I will not receive the evidence of a man with whom I am not on terms. That's the law, I believe? (*To* QUILT.)

QUILT. That is the law.

O'H. Thank you, Dick. Dick Quilt, that man's a villain (*indicating* ROLLESTONE). If he says you've committed a burglary, don't you believe him.

QUILT (*contemptuously*). Captain O'Hara, I wouldn't believe that fellow on his oath!

O'H. (*shaking hands with* QUILT). Thank you, Dick— thank you. God bless you. (*To Keepers.*) Remove the prisoner; the case is adjourned (*exeunt Keepers with* QUILT). And now, sir, that you and I are alone, perhaps you'll tell me what you mean by secretly ensnaring the affections of my niece?

ROL. (*aside*). I suppose there's nothing for it but to face it out! (*Aloud.*) My dear O'Hara, don't be too hard upon me. Now I ask you, as a fine impressionable, susceptible old sea-dog, with a keen eye for a pretty girl—come, you know you have that—who would know your niece without falling in love with her? Is is fair to expect a simple, loving, impulsive, affectionate nature like mine to be a match for the astonishing aggregate of charms with which that young lady is endowed.

O'H. There's something in that. It isn't the falling in love with her that I find fault with—that's natural. It's the sneaking, underhand way in which you've, so to speak, circumnavigated her innocent young heart. I'll never see her again—never.

ROL. Nonsense! Don't be unjust to the girl. It was my fault; *she* couldn't help it. Now, I ask you, is it fair to expect a young and inexperienced girl to be proof against the battery of wily resource that such a practised hand as I am can bring to bear upon her?

O'H. There's a good deal of truth in that. You're a deuced good-looking fellow, confound you!

Rol. No, no!

O'H. But I say you are.

Rol. Very good, have it your own way—only, mind you, I don't agree with you.

O'H. Never mind. I can forgive *her*. You've got an uncommon flow of small talk. Hang it, sir, you're a very pleasant companion!

Rol. Not at all.

O'H. (*furious*). But, confound it, I say you are! And a devilish clever fellow too! Perhap's you'll contradict *that?*

Rol. No—I'm devilish clever!

O'H. Ah! I thought we should get to something in time. Why even *I* liked you! Hang it, I was very fond of you! And if you'd only been open and aboveboard, I'd have given my right hand to see you spliced to my girl. But you shall marry her—do you hear me? You shall marry her, or, by George, I'll commit you for Breach of Promise. I'm a magistrate, and I know the law.

Rol. (*aside*). This is getting rather too warm to be pleasant. Never mind—I'm in the hands of Destiny —she can do what she likes with me. I've begun it— I must go on with it.

O'H. Now, I ask you, Jeff Rollestone, are you prepared to marry her, yes or no?

Rol. Marry her? To be sure I am.

O'H. But at once—at once?

Rol. Of course—why not? She's single, isn't she?

O'H. Single? Yes! (*Puzzled*). You're a most remarkable man. Why didn't you say you were ready to marry her at first?

Rol. Didn't I say it ? I believe you're right. I did *not* say it. It—it escaped me.

O'H. Well, if you're going to do the right thing by her—that puts a different aspect on affairs. Why, my bird is the very wife for a good-for-nothing idle scape-grace like you. I've said so, over and over again. Snake hands, Jeff Rollestone. I'm sorry I was hasty.

Rol. Not at all—don't name it. (*Aside.*) I don't know, Destiny, where you're driving to, but I suppose you know all about it.

O'H. But, I say, I hear you've given up your secretaryship ?

Rol. Yes. I—I've given that up.

O'H. It's a singular thing, but when Mr. Seton's secretaries are kicked out of their berths, they always come and propose for my niece. Have you got any money ?

Rol. Four and sixpence. Seton owes me a sovereign.

O'H. Whew ! That's not enough- Never mind. I'm a warm man. I've saved money, and we'll all live here together.

Rol. Certainly, if Edith has no objection.

O'H. Edith ?

Rol. I mean your niece.

O'H. Her name is Jessie.

Rol. Edith is French for Jessie.

O'H. Never knew that before. But why did she keep all this from me ?

Rol. Oh, I insisted on it.

O'H. Why ?

Rol. Exactly. I often ask myself that. I say to myself, " Why not be open and above-board ? Why deceive the old man ? Why not declare everything ? She loves you - -" By-the-bye, she *does* love me, doesn't she ?

O'H.   Love you ?   Why look at her letter !   (*producing it.*)

ROL.   Exactly ; *you've* read it, *I* haven't.   " She loves you——"   Shall we say fondly ?

O'H.   (*Referring to letter.*)   Yes ; I should say fondly.

ROL.   Exactly, fondly.   Then why not admit it ? That is the question that I am continually putting to myself, and, upon my word and honour, without any result of any kind whatever.

O'H.   Jeff. Rollestone, was there ever any madness in your family ?

ROL.   I don't know.   My grandfather was a hatter in a large way of business.

O'H.   I thought as much.   Well, say no more about it, you're a right good chap, and I'm as pleased as Punch.   Lord bless you, I love a wedding, and betwixt you and me—betwixt you and me, I say—I don't know but what I mayn't be having one of my own, one of these days !   Ha ! ha ! ha !   [*Exit* O'HARA.

ROL.   (*looking after him*) There are certain situations in which a man feels tempted to ask himself, why the Devil he was born ?   I'm sure I don't know, I didn't want to be born.   I took no steps to bring it about.   I was there, but I wasn't consulted ; it's one of those liberties that parents *do* take with their children—they presume on their relationship.   Here I am—five and thirty years old—half my life gone—best half, too—and except a suit of clothes, four and sixpence and a moustache, pretty well where I was when I began it !   So it all ends !   Back from the quiet peaceful time of hard work and dawning self-respect—back from the glimpse of what might have been—back to the old misery—the old squalor—the old ragged dog-life, with its ever-present shame and ceaseless self-reproach !   Gerard, old man, when this tale is told to you in the rough, you

will kick me out of your heart for a graceless hound
who used the position you gave him to try and rob you
of the woman you were to marry. So be it—I am sick
of fighting against long odds. When you and she have
been happy together for many years, and the old tur-
bulent time of active love and feverish jealousy is left far
behind, perhaps she will tell you all about the poor
luckless devil who loved her so well—and who broke
his heart for both of you! Broke his heart? The
drivel of boys and girls! Time's rough usage should
have woven a pretty tough cuticle about my weather
worn anatomy, by this time!

Enter Miss Parminter.

Miss P. Capt. O'Hara—I am quite ready when you
are (*starts on seeing* Rollestone), Mr. Rollestone! I
am pained and surprised to find you still here.

Rol. Miss Parminter—I am afraid my conduct
must appear very odd and inexplicable to you.

Miss P. No, sir—you are but as I have found that
most men are— you think it no shame to try and trifle
with a simple woman's most sacred emotions—to you
it is but a pleasant means of whiling away a trivial
hour—you little think that the tune you have idly
thrummed upon her very heartstrings may have incor-
porated itself into her very existence. But so it is, Mr.
Rollestone—so, but too often, it is! (*sobbing*).

Rol. Miss Parminter, you have been kind and good to
me, and I cannot bear that you should think so ill of
me. I am not a heartless scoundrel—if you knew all
you would not say so. I am going from Drumferry for
ever; but before I go I should like to put myself right,
at least with you. For I am very heavy-hearted, and
I think you might say that which would at least send
me away in a happier frame of mind.

72

Miss P. (*much agitated*). Go on—I am listening.

Rol. The good and gifted woman of whom you speak, I have loved as I shall never love again. After the disclosure of last night, I fear that I have for ever forfeited her esteem. My mouth is closed, and I may not explain. But whether she thinks well or ill of me, that love I shall carry in my heart to the end of my life. Will you believe this of me, Miss Parminter? (*Taking her hand.*)

Miss P. (*deeply moved*). Mr. Rollestone—Jeffery—(*he seems much surprised at this form of address*)—call me weak —foolish, if you will, but—I *do* believe you! You are pardoned! I know what young men are. I have studied them earnestly and devotedly; and no true woman who knows them, and who loves earnestly, and with all her heart, can be severe on what is, after all, but a too common type of youthful folly. I may *grieve* for a lifetime, but I cannot *frown* for a day. Are you happy, Jeffery?

Rol. (*embarrassed*). But—I beg your pardon—its an awkward thing to have to say--but I can't help thinking—its an extremely difficult and delicate thing to say—but I can't help thinking that you have entirely misunderstood me.

Miss P. (*alarmed*). I have misunderstood you?

Rol. Yes. I have the very highest respect and regard for you, Miss Parminter—the very highest regard—you have always been most kind to me, and— I am extremely sorry to have been so awkward as to have misled you, in any way—its quite unpardonable--but I never aspired to be more than a very sincere and true friend to you, I—I was referring to Mrs. Callendar!

Miss P. (*with a violent effort to repress her mortification*) So was I!

ROL. Indeed? I was mad enough to think—but your enthusiasm on behalf of your friend, misled me, and I fancied—(*aside*)—this is deuced awkward!

MISS P. (*still speaking with an effort*). I am an enthusiast. It is foolish of me, but I can quite understand your mistake. I—I should have been more guarded (*goes to door*). Marion, my love!

ROL. (*hurriedly*). Miss Parminter, pray, spare me!

MISS P. Marion, my love—I want you, for one moment.

Enter MARION. *She starts on seeing* ROLLESTONE.

MARION. Miss Parminter! I had no idea of this; This is very cruel of you.

MISS P. (*almost hysterical*). No, my dear, it isn't. You wouldn't say so, if you knew all. Mr. Rollestone is very sorry for the pain he caused you—he has told me so—he can explain his conduct—he has told me so —he never loved anybody but you—he has told me so—and I'm a silly old fool (*crying*), and I ought to have known better; and - and he has told me so! But don't say I'm cruel to you—you wouldn't say that, if you knew what has just passed—you wouldn't, indeed —oh, you wouldn't, indeed!

[*Exit* MISS PARMINTER *sobbing*.

RO . Believe me, Marion, I did not seek this meeting.

MAR. (*whose manner is hard, and cold, and matter-of-fact*). I can quite believe that, Mr. Rolleston; but now that we have met, is it not better to come to an understanding? We misled one another yesterday, did we not? The recollection of what had been gave an artificial vitality to emotion that, for all practical purposes had died out long ago. A night's reflection has proved that to me and, no doubt, to you also.

ROL. (*despondently*). Yes! It is a pity that our old regard for one another was ever referred to between us.

MAR. A thousand pities. As you said yesterday, all that is at an end, and we see how foolish—how very foolish we were, and how right my mother was to separate us. For we did not know one another.

ROL. Marion, I have nothing to say—my mouth is closed. But have pity on me—I don't ask for more than that. Oh, Marion, my heart is almost gone, and hope is well-nigh dead within me!

MAR. I am sorry to hear that, because I have something of a very earnest character to say to you. This girl—this poor girl, whose letter you laid claim to last night, you will act honourably towards her, will you not? You will not take all this wealth of love from her, and give her nothing in return? Above all, you will never let her know that you have played a double game with her, for if she loves you, as it would seem that she does, that will break her heart.

ROL. You are very hard on me, but I cannot complain. I ask but one mercy of you, that you will leave me alone in my misery. The old life is before me, and I can face it. For God's sake let me go to my ruin my own way. Tell me that I have deceived you—that my professed constancy was a lie—that the story of my wasted life was a miserable hypocrisy—that I am but a shallow and hollow-hearted double-dealer, who looks upon such women as you, and such love as yours, as the playthings of an hour. Tell me this, and have done with me. Think of me as you will, but in mercy leave me to myself!

MAR. Mercy? What mercy have I received from you? Now listen to me, Jeffery Rollestone. I have seen the man upon whom that letter was found, he has told me a truth which you, for some reason of your own,

thought fit to keep from me. That letter was written to Gerard Seton.

Rol. Marion, I——.

Mar. Hear me out. For a reason which I do not care to inquire into, you thought it prudent to weigh your regard for my cousin against your love for me, and that love has been found wanting. Well, I am content to have been warned in time. I am content to think that I might have learnt this too late. I am content to adopt your words of yesterday, and to say with you, we did not know one another, indeed!

Rol. Marion, to Gerard Seton I owed everything that I then possessed. In the blindness of his faith, in the utter kindliness of his kindly nature, he took me by the hand and raised me to the position I had forfeited. I learnt then that his hopes and the hopes of his house rested on his gaining your love. Was it for me to turn his good deed against himself? Was it for me, who owed him all, to take all from him?

Mar. You acted blindly. Three months since he would have married me. I then told him that I believed it could never be. Within a week I wrote to him telling him that he must never think of me as his wife, for (*with emotion*), oh, Jeffery, I had seen you, and the love that slept had wakened into life! I was very sorry for him, for he had been to me as a brother, but my sorrow was wasted. (*Bitterly.*) He bore the blow bravely, indeed, for now he has a wife.

Rol. Oh, forgive me—oh, forgive me! Marion— my own old love—have pity on the weak man who strove to be strong! Have pity on the idle, self-indulgent outcast, who, in the fulness of his gratitude, sought for duty and thought he had found it!

Mar. (*softened*). Had *I* no claim on this gratitude? See of what a treasure you would have robbed me : see into what a life-long sorrow you would have plunged me! I, who had given you all that was in me. I, who loved you utterly and beyond all on earth!

ROL. God bless you, Marion, for the hope that is within me, and for the life that is before me? (*Embrace*).

Enter GERARD SETON.

GER. (*surprised*). Jeff. Rollestone— Marion? I—— (*hesitating, then recovering himself*). Come, I have nothing to conceal from *you*. I have news for you—guess what it is?

MAR. That the deadly wound I inflicted has healed over? That I have reverted to my old condition of a cousin with the brevet rank of sister? That, knowing that I would not give you pain without giving pain to myself, you thought the best way of proving that I need have no anxiety on my account, was to marry a wife?

GER. (*taken aback*). I thought I should have astonished *you*, but, by Jove! you have astonished *me*. Yes, that's my news.

MAR. Well, it was very self-denying of you to make so great a sacrifice on my account. And when shall I have the pleasure of making Mrs. Gerard Seton's acquaintance?

GER. Without a moment's delay. (*goes to door*). My darling! (JESSIE *enters timidly*). This is my wife, Marion.

MAR. (*surprised.*) Why it's Jessie O'Hara? I don't think so much of your self-denial after all. (*Kisses her*).

ROL. (*interested*). Jessie O'Hara? Dear me, is this Jessie O'Hara? I—I take a great interest in Jessie O'Hara. In fact, it's rather awkward, but this young lady is engaged to be married to *me*. (JESSIE *surprised*).

GER. Some mistake, I think?

Rol. No, there's no mistake. You've treated me very badly, Jessie, very badly indeed ; but under the circum-stances I forgive you. Is there any objection to my forgiving her on the cheek ? Thank you. (*Kisses her.*)

Jes. (*to* Gerard), I'm sure I don't know what he means !

Mar. But, does Capt. O'Hara know that you are married ?

Jes. Yes. Mrs. Callendar—I telegraphed to him last night to tell him, and that I should be with him this morning.

Ger. We kept it secret for fear of my father's anger. But Lord Dunveggan, his cousin, died suddenly yester-day, leaving a will in his favour, and the Drumferry mortgages can be paid off as soon as his Lordship's executors please.

Rol. Gerard, you have robbed me of a very charm-ing little wife—but I'm even with you after all. (*kissing* Marion).

Ger. (*surprised*) Why you don't mean to tell me—

Rol. I *did'nt* mean to tell you—but under the cir-cumstances I don't see why I shouldn't.

Ger. My dear Marion—I can't tell you how de-lighted I am—you have the love of a much better fellow than I am, and one who will make you a much better husband.

Jes. A much better husband ?

Ger. (*taken aback*) Ha—hum—a much better *looking* husband, Jessie.

Jes. I don't agree with you at all.

Ger. Then let me see—Marion is the——

Rol. The old love of whom I told you. The hope of the old days has come to pass—the misery of ten years goes for nothing, and there is no happier man in the world !

Enter O'HARA, MISS PARMINTER, *and* MR. SETON.
O'HARA *has an open telegram in his hand.*

O'H. I should think not, my boy—I should think not ! A pretty wife don't fall to a man's lot every day in the week !

MISS P. I should hope not, indeed, Captain O'Hara. It is only under the most imperfect form of civilization that such a state of things could be possible.

O'H. And take my word for it, Jeff Rollestone, she's as good as she's pretty. There isn't a better girl in the country, though I say it who shouldn't.

ROL. Not say it ? Why shouldn't you say it ? Its a pleasant thing to hear, from whomsoever it may come. Not that I wanted any assurance of it, for I've loved her these ten years.

O'H. Ten years ? You dont say so. The slyness of some people. Why didn't you tell me all about it ? But never mind that now, you must congratulate *me*, I've been driving in a gig to Drumferry (*significantly*) with Miss Parminter.

ROL. Well, what of that ?

O'H. Nothing, only that a man who drives with Miss Parminter in a gig is a very lucky fellow—that's all—eh, Clara ? (*turning to Miss Parminter*).

MISS P. Let us quit the flowery but uncertain paths of metaphor, which begin very well, but land us goodness only knows where ; in a matter of so much moment, one cannot be too distinct. It is possible that Captain O'Hara may, in time, win both my hand and my heart !

MR. S. My dear Clara, I congratulate you with all my heart.

ROLLESTON *has been talking affectionately to* MARION.

O'H. I say—Jeff Rollestone— hang it all—not before Jessie !

ROL. Oh she won't mind—she's a married woman.

O'II. I know she's a married woman, but that's just why she *will* mind. Its rather soon to begin that sort of thing, isn't it ?

RoL. What sort of thing ?

O.H. When *I* was a young man, a decent husband only did that sort of thing, when his wife's back was turned. Never mind, Jessie, my bird—*I'll* keep him straight.

Jes. Keep Mr. Rollestone straight, uncle ? I think Mrs. Callendar may be trusted to do that.

O.H. Mrs. Callendar !

RoL. Yes, O'Hara. I am going to be married to Mrs. Callendar.

O'H. You villain ! But you shan't marry her—I'll commit you for Breach of Promise—I'm a magistrate, and I know the law. Jessie, my love, don't cry—he *shall* marry you.

Jes. (*laughing*). But uncle, I don't think he *can* marry me, for I am married already.

O'H. Married ? To whom ?

Jes. To Mr. Seton.

(O'Hara *turns in astonishment to old* Mr. Seton).

Mr. Seton. Not to me, Captain O'Hara. I am not so fortunate. To my son.

Jes. Why you have my telegram in your hand.

O'H. (*looking at it*). Jessie Seton, born O'Hara, next time you telegraph to me to say you have been and married somebody, perhaps, to save mistakes, you'll be ⌄ good enough to say who you've married.

Ger. But surely the letter that fell into your hands —the last letter that I received from Jessie—must have made *that* quite clear to you.

O'H. That letter made it clear ? As a source of fog and general bedevilment, the Banks of Newfoundland are a fool to it.

Rol. Then let me clear the fog away. I took upon myself the ownership of that letter in the belief that in doing so I was helping to extract your niece and my friend from a very serious dilemma. That I was mistaken, only goes to show that there is no duty paramount to that which a man owes to a worthy woman who blesses him with her true and blameless love. That love, when it was mine, was the mainspring of my life. When that love went from me I died a social death. Marion, you have called me to life again—that life is in your keeping, and with it my honour, my courage, my manhood, and my love.

CURTAIN.

www.ingramcontent.com/pod-product-compliance
Lightning Source LLC
Chambersburg PA
CBHW021118020726
47500CB00003B/824